PRAISE FOR BOOKS BY MARGI PREUS

Heart of a Samurai
NEWBERY HONOR BOOK

★ "It's a classic fish-out-of-water story . . .
and it's precisely this classic structure that gives the novel
the sturdy bones of a timeless tale."
—*Booklist*, starred review

★ "Stunning debut novel."
—*School Library Journal*, starred review

★ "Preus succeeds in making readers feel every bit
as 'other' as Manjiro, while showing America at its best
and worst through his eyes."
—*Publishers Weekly*, starred review

West of the Moon

★ "Preus interweaves the mesmerizing tale
of Astri's treacherous and harrowing mid-nineteenth-century
emigration to America with bewitching tales of magic."
—*Booklist*, starred review

★ "History, fiction and folklore intertwine seamlessly
in this lively, fantastical adventure and moving coming-of-age story."
—*Kirkus Reviews*, starred review

★ "Several Norwegian folktales are seamlessly integrated
into the fast-paced, lyrically narrated story, which features
a protagonist as stalwart and fearless as any fairy-tale hero."
—*Horn Book*, starred review

MARGI PREUS

AMULET BOOKS
NEW YORK

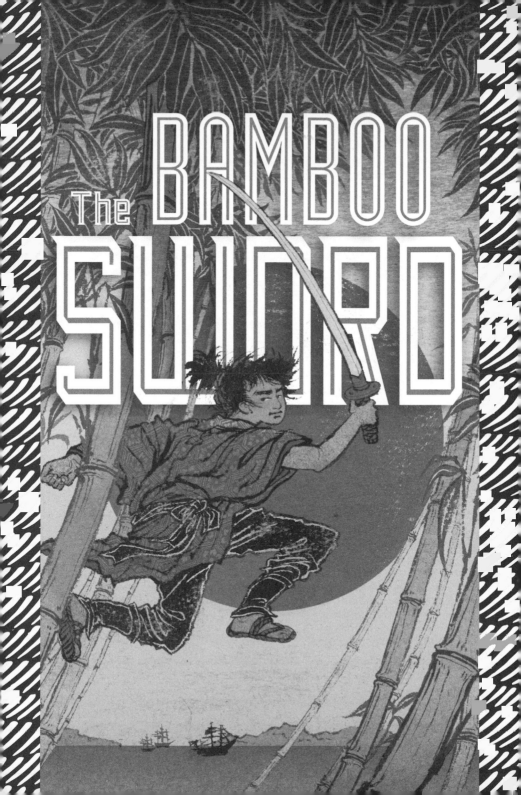

The Library of Congress has catalogued the hardcover edition of this book as follows:

Preus, Margi.
The bamboo sword / Margi Preus.
pages cm
Includes bibliographical references.
ISBN 978-1-4197-0807-7 (hardback)
[1. Adventure and adventurers—Fiction. 2. Americans—Japan—Fiction.
3. Friendship—Fiction. 4. Seafaring life—Fiction. 5. Samurai—Fiction.
6. Nakahama, Manjiro, 1827–1898—Fiction. 7. Perry, Matthew
Calbraith, 1794–1858—Fiction. 8. Japan—History—Restoration,
1853–1870—Fiction.] I. Title.
PZ7.P92434Bam 2015
[Fic]—dc23
2015002063

ISBN for this edition: 978-1-4197-0824-4

Text copyright © 2015 Margi Preus
Illustrations on pages v–ix, 18, 22, 264 copyright © 2015 Yuko Shimizu
Book design by Chad W. Beckerman

Printed and bound in U.S.A.
10 9 8 7 6 5 4 3 2 1

Amulet Books are available at special discounts when purchased in quantity for premiums and promotions as well as fundraising or educational use. Special editions can also be created to specification. For details, contact specialsales@abramsbooks.com or the address below.

ABRAMS The Art of Books
115 West 18th Street, New York, NY 10011
abramsbooks.com

What is constant in this world of change?

Yesterday.

—Anonymous Japanese poem

CONTENTS

PART ONE WATER

PART TWO EARTH

PART THREE WIND

PART FOUR FIRE

PART FIVE AIR

PART ONE
WATER

We make water our model and turn our mind into water.
Water adjusts itself to a square or round vessel with ease.
It can turn itself into a single droplet or into a vast ocean.
—Miyamoto Musashi, *The Book of Five Rings*

1

BLACK DRAGONS
BELCHING SMOKE

3rd Day of the 6th Month of the 6th Year of
the Era of Long Happiness (July 8, 1853)

Yoshi was a leaf, spinning in the summer breeze. He was
water running over stones. He was the thin, free air.

Or at least that was what he tried to be. But, really, he
was just Yoshi, spinning, lunging, twisting, and slashing. The
sword he imagined flashing in his hands was only a length of
bamboo. His blade did not exactly flash, but it was at least
burnished by the early morning sunlight.

He kept his heels slightly off the ground so as to move
quickly, but he could never quite capture the graceful, gliding
motions of the teacher. No matter how much he practiced, he
still felt awkward. His slow moves weren't smooth enough, his
fast moves not quick enough. *More practice*, he told himself.

Under the flickering green leaves, with the sound of the
rushing brook in his ears, Yoshi started again. But something, he
wasn't sure what, made him drop his arm, stand still, and listen.

Except for the brook and the silvery call of a bird, it was quiet. A familiar quiet, old as these hills and the nearby temple, old as the silent stone Buddha who watched him at his sword practice. But now he noticed that there *was* a sound, a kind of dull thumping, as if his heart were beating somewhere outside his body. It was so faint that it was almost not a sound.

He walked to the rocky outcropping that overlooked the village and the bay beyond. A humid haze hung over the valley, made thicker by the smoke from cooking fires. In the village, women were just now rising to begin making their families' breakfasts. He slid his hand into the fold of his sleeve and felt the cold rice ball wrapped in a radish leaf.

Should he eat some? Or save it? He was hungry now, so perhaps now would be a good time. But he would be hungry later, too, and it was painful to watch the other boys eat while he had nothing. He pulled his hand away. He could wait.

Beyond the village, the blue water of the bay winked in the early morning sun. Boats were just leaving the harbor for a day of fishing, their sails bright against the dark hills. Every day the water in the bay looked different: black under glowering clouds, or blue as the daimyo's silk kimono. Some days it moved as if it were alive, rippling like a horse's flank.

Why was it that the water could change every day, but absolutely nothing else ever did? The village below—its thatched roofs and bamboo fences, the skinny stray dogs that trotted along the dirt roads—it had all been like this for hundreds of years and would be forever more, as far as Yoshi could tell. These ancient hills and the temples hidden in them had stood for thousands of years, and probably would for thousands more.

And yet, this morning, something seemed different. It was as if everything—the village, the hills beyond, the early morning mist and the smoke from cooking fires, the last reverberation of the temple bell, even the water in the bay— everything seemed to be holding its breath.

The only sound was the steady thumping Yoshi had noticed earlier, and which had grown closer. Yoshi now recognized it as a runner's soft, thudding footfall. Next the runner himself appeared, a man dressed in a short kimono and a lacquer hat who raced along the path toward the daimyo's dwelling place. The man glanced at Yoshi as he ran past. "You'd better hang on to your 'sword,' little 'samurai,'" he panted.

"What?" Yoshi said. "Why?"

"In the bay!" the man called over his shoulder. "Black dragons belching smoke!"

What a crazy person! Yoshi thought, but when he turned back to glance at the valley one more time, he saw something he had not noticed before. Far down the bay, toward the ocean, puffs of black smoke rose into the air.

2

THROWING ROCKS
AT THE SUN

On the way to Hideki's dojo, Yoshi carried the slippers his young master would wear later in his indoor classes, and an extra pair of wooden clogs in case of wet weather. He walked slightly behind and to the side of Hideki. On the other side was the umbrella bearer, Jun, who shielded the young samurai's head from the hot sun.

Hideki had turned fifteen the previous year, and he now wore the samurai's daisho: the two swords, one long and one short. As they walked along the dirt road to the school, Hideki clicked his fingers against the hilt of his katana, something he shouldn't do. Perhaps he was still having trouble getting used to the swords, Yoshi thought.

Yoshi knew he should not look left or right but instead keep his eyes straight ahead. Still, he couldn't help craning his neck to see if anything unusual was happening.

"What is it, Yoshitaro?" Hideki asked kindly, using Yoshi's full name. "Are you looking for something?"

"Please excuse my foolishness," Yoshi said, lowering his

eyes. Had anyone else seen the black smoke? he wondered. Should he say something to Hideki? He chewed on his lip, trying to decide what to do with the strange information he had. He imagined a dozen different ways of explaining what he'd seen and heard, but every one of them sounded outlandish. Unbelievable. Ridiculous. He would sound like a crazy person. Nobody would believe him, not even Hideki.

In the entryway to the dojo, Hideki stepped out of his wooden sandals, which Yoshi bowed to, picked up, and bowed to again before placing them into their special shoe compartment. Meanwhile, Jun collapsed the umbrella and tucked it into the umbrella compartment.

Yoshi helped Hideki into the quilted, bamboo-lined vest, the face shield, and the other protective gear that he wore when at practice. Then Hideki stood with his left arm stiff by his side while Yoshi tied the arm to his body. Swords were worn on the left side, and so a bushi had to draw and fight with the right hand. This was the law from ancient times.

Unfortunately, Hideki was not naturally right-handed, and he was having difficulty learning to fight the correct way. Sometimes Yoshi wished he could take Hideki's place and spare him the embarrassment he suffered for his clumsiness. But the only kindness he could offer was to avoid Hideki's eyes while he tied the knots binding his master's arm to his side.

When Hideki and the other samurai went into the courtyard to practice, Yoshi and Jun retreated into a grove of shade trees with the other servants. Most of them pulled paper-wrapped snacks from their sleeves. Yoshi turned away and went to find a place where he could keep an eye on Hideki and maybe observe some of the action in the class.

Jun trotted after him. "Oh, brother," he said. "Look who's here."

Yoshi turned to see the man everyone called Kitsune—the Fox—who was the head of the family's bodyguards. Jun and Yoshi tried to avoid Kitsune as much as possible, for it was said that he used his sword more often than his tongue.

This morning, though, he was using his tongue to complain about the way the kendo master ran the class.

"These boys are soft!" he groused to his friend as they stood with crossed arms, watching. "They only ever practice with bamboo sticks! They should be testing their swords on corpses and practicing archery on dogs, as we did in our training years."

"Well," Kitsune's companion said, laughing, "at least as our *grandfathers* did."

Yoshi's stomach turned. He sometimes imagined that he

might be a samurai. But even if he really were, he would not shoot dogs!

"In this next exercise, we will say that the two opponents are in the following positions," the sword master was saying. Yoshi turned his attention to him.

Behind Yoshi, Jun yawned and said, "Time for a nap!" He stretched out under a ginkgo tree. "How about you?"

"Maybe in a bit," Yoshi said.

"Don't get any big ideas, Yoshitaro-san," Jun teased. "You'll never be a bushi, you know, no matter how much you eavesdrop on their lessons."

"I know, but . . ." Yoshi bit his tongue and turned his attention back to the instructor, who was showing how to knock an opponent's sword away. The teacher made it look easy, demonstrating with one of the students.

"You're like the boy who throws rocks at the sun," Jun joked.

"Uh-huh," Yoshi said absently. The instructor was demonstrating another move, using a real blade. Yoshi loved to watch the teacher's graceful moves, the curving lines, the smooth, perfect steel—the way man and sword became one fluid, lethal dancer.

Later, alone in the forest, Yoshi would practice what he had observed. He would try to move in the teacher's slow, sure, meditative way, then dart, fast as a snake, to wound his imaginary opponent.

"You're funny," Jun said. "You're the only one watching. Even his students don't pay attention to him."

It was true. The students who were waiting their turns lolled in the heat, their heads drooping. Some of them who waited outside were dozing under the trees, the shade hiding their closed eyes.

"They're all bored," Jun said. "What do they need to learn this for, anyway? There hasn't been a war for hundreds of years."

"I suppose you're right," Yoshi replied. "But what if there *was* one?"

"A war with whom?" Jun said. "The shogun has complete power. He keeps the families of the lords in Edo, as if they were hostages, so they can't rebel. The only time samurai ever use their swords is to test their sharpness on corpses. Or on poor peasants like us."

"What if the barbarians from the West should come?" Yoshi said.

Jun scoffed. "Barbarians! If they come, our warriors will run them through—one, two, three!" He slapped his hands together as if cleaning them off. "The things you think! Why do you waste your time with such worry?" He closed his eyes.

Everything Jun said was true. Yoshi and Jun would never

carry swords, never put on battle armor, never ride a horse into war, even if there was one. Still, he couldn't help but watch the sword master's graceful movements, mentally imitating them, while wondering why *did* he waste his time learning things he could never use? It was like Jun said, as senseless as throwing rocks at the sun.

As he pondered this, a horse and rider thundered into the courtyard. The rider glanced around and, apparently deciding that Kitsune was the highest-ranked samurai there, dismounted, ran to him, and, bowing, gasped his breathless message: "Foreign ships in the harbor—black ships that move without sails! Alien ships of fire! The country is about to be invaded by a hundred thousand white devils! All samurai are to prepare for battle!"

A Japanese artist's interpretation of a Black Ship. (*artist unknown*)

3

ABOARD THE *SUSQUEHANNA*

Friday, July 8, 1853

*As the ships neared the bay, signals were made from the Commodore,
and instantly the decks were cleared for action, the guns placed in position
and shotted, the ammunition arranged, the small arms made ready,
sentinels and men at their posts, and, in short, all the preparations made,
usual before meeting an enemy.*

—M. C. Perry, *Narrative of the Expedition
to the China Seas and Japan, 1852–1854*

Jack had only just glimpsed the peaks of Japan when the
order rang out: "General quarters!" The drums began their
steady roll, the thrum coming from all four ships: the two steam
frigates, the *Susquehanna* and the *Mississippi*, and the two sloops
of war, the *Saratoga* and the *Plymouth*. It seemed that even Jack's
heart drummed out the rhythm, a relentless roll, punctuated by
sharp, pounding beats.

The deck came alive with men lowering sails, stowing gear,

and running to their stations. Boxes of shot were uncovered, the great guns run out, cannonballs heaped beside each cannon.

Jack tried to steal glances at the lush, green hills and rocky cliffs as he made his way to his assigned place: gun number four. A loose chicken scuttled past him, squawking among the chaos.

"Flapjacket!" a midshipman barked at him. "Secure that wayward hen!"

Jack veered after the renegade chicken, dived, grabbed her by the feet, and crammed her into the coop, then raced to the gun deck, where the orders were already flying:

"Pile that shot up neat."

"Uncover that box of grape."

"Pry open that case of canister shot."

All these orders came at once and from three different people. It was always this way. As a lowly cabin boy, Jack took orders from everyone, and there was always something he was supposed to be doing that he was not, and always somewhere he was supposed to be where he was not. He helped the cook in the galley, served the officers, carried messages, scrambled into the rigging to clear a halyard, stood watch, and most regularly was assigned to tend the chickens and the livestock and clean their coops and pens. The only one lowlier was Willis: smallest, skinniest, and shyest.

If the need arose, it was up to the two of them, Jack and

Willis, to be powder monkeys, ferrying gunpowder from the powder magazine to the gun deck—but only in case of actual battle. Still, at every drill, they were required to *pretend* to carry their lethal cargo from the lower deck to the guns. This time, though, there was the possibility of real battle, and Jack felt a tremor of excitement run through him.

When every gun was readied, everything in place, and every man at his station, a deathly silence fell over the ship. All stood at full attention as the four ships made their steady way up the bay at nine knots, puffing out their clouds of black smoke.

Jack stood on an overturned bucket, peering over the bulwark at the terraced valleys, towns, and villages undulating past. An offshore breeze carried with it the smell of green, growing things. It was so delicious, Jack could almost taste it.

How often had he dreamed of this exotic, unknown region of the world, hoping that by some enchantment he might be wafted here. And now here he was, Jack Sullivan, among the first to see this land, closed to outside eyes for the past 250 years. And for all those years, this country, so far as anyone knew, had lived in peace. What other nation could say the same? Certainly not the United States, which had been in some kind of war ever since the revolution that had started it seventy-five years earlier.

"Do you suppose people who live in a country that is never at war are different from people who live in a country that is constantly at war?" Jack mused. He turned to Willis, who blinked at him, his pale eyelashes fluttering nervously. "It certainly seems peaceful here," Jack went on. The countryside, enveloped by a delicate gray haze, was tranquillity itself.

The *Susquehanna* was anything but. Its decks bristled with muskets and men armed with carbines, pistols, and cutlasses. Sentinels were stationed fore and aft, and neat piles of round shot and four stands of grape stood ready beside each gun.

Suddenly, a battery from land puffed a cloud of white smoke, and everyone on deck tensed, waiting for the explosion. But instead of the expected missile, a rocket burst in the air.

"'Tis but a signal," Griggs, the grizzled old captain of the gun, announced.

"Will they be hostile or peaceable, d'ye suppose?" asked Ramsey, the rammer and sponger.

"As to the manner of our reception, there is nothing certain," answered Davis, first loader.

"Orders are 'Any unusu'l movement on shore or on the water, sound the alarm,'" Griggs said. "Boats're not allowed to approach within rifle range. We're t' meet force with force."

"I say we blow all the slant-eyes to the heavens," Toley, another cabin boy, grumbled. "They're naught but heathens anyhow. Ain't I right, Willis?" He smiled at Willis, which, Jack knew, was Willis's cue to agree.

Willis didn't answer right away.

"Am I right, Willis?" Toley asked again, his smile tightening.

"Right," Willis muttered.

Jack wondered if it didn't irk Willis to always have to agree with everything Toley said. But maybe Willis didn't mind. He never said he did.

"The commodore says our mission is to 'bring a singular and isolated people into the family of civilized nations,'" Ramsey quoted.

"I'll tell you the real reason we're here," said Davis. "It's trade we're after. To get some ports where American ships might land. Whalers, merchants, and the like. And to get coal to keep our steamers running."

"They wants nothin' to do with us, I tell ye!" Griggs insisted. "We've all heard their edick what says, 'So long as the sun shall warm th' earth, let no Christian be so bold as to come to Japan; and let all know that the king of Spain, or the Christian's God, or the great God on all, if he should get it in his mind to come here, shall pay for it with his head.'"

"From what I've heard," said Smith, one of the topmen, getting into the conversation, "they'll have to go along with our demands. There's those that think we could load all their cannon into one of our sixty-four-pounders and shoot them all back!"

"Maybe so," Griggs went on, his voice becoming a low growl.

"But ne'er forget, they be masters of the cold steel. 'Tis said their blades're bright and sharp and can cleave a man asunder from head to foot."

Ramsey nodded solemnly, then added, "Aye, and they slice so cleanly from shoulder to crotch that a man'll walk on several paces afore falling in two!"

There was silence as all pondered on that.

Jack's heart was as heavy as if it had been packed with grapeshot. Where had all his earlier bravado gone? All the way from Macao to Japan, he—and the others, too—had bragged about how many heathens they would knock off if it came to a fight. Jack had buzzed with excitement at the prospect of getting to be a powder monkey in the thick of the action. Wouldn't that be something to tell his friends back home? He'd tell them about the real fighting he'd been in and how he'd blown the heads off a few of those slant-eyed devils.

Now, though, faced with the actual possibility of having fire directed back at them, and hearing tales of the Japanese swords, the buzz of excitement turned to a kind of rolling beat—farther back in his head, in the back of his throat, and thrumming away like a drum beating to quarters in the pit of his stomach.

4

THE ARMOR

The courtyard came suddenly alive. The young samurai roused themselves from the shade of the trees and stood blinking in the bright sunlight as the kendo teacher shouted instructions at them.

Kitsune stalked across the courtyard and addressed Yoshi and Jun: "Tell the house servants to make preparations, and to ready Hideki's armor." When the boys didn't move, he added, "Don't just stand there! Go!"

Yoshi and Jun turned and ran.

At Hideki's dwelling, wind chimes clinked and clanged in lonely fashion. It seemed like the only sound in the whole house, except for old Chuu, who was solemnly sweeping the entryway.

"Where is everyone?" Yoshi asked.

"Family members are in their chambers, making preparations. Some servants ran away," Chuu said. "Afraid of the white devils."

"Why haven't you run away?" Jun asked.

16

Chuu tapped the broom handle against his bad leg. "Can't run," he said.

"What should we do?" Jun wondered aloud. "Maybe we should run away, too."

"And tomorrow morning not have our jobs?" Yoshi said. "Or, worse, our heads?"

"Aren't you worried about the barbarians?"

"I'm more worried about the wrath of Kitsune than I am about the barbarians," Yoshi said. "I think we'd better find and prepare Hideki's armor ourselves." His fingers twitched with the anticipation of actually touching real armor.

The boys found the large chest that held Hideki's armor and opened it. The smell of mildew knocked Yoshi back for a moment.

"Here it is," he said. "He inherited his grandfather's armor or something like that. I remember hearing about it."

"Ohhh . . . ," Jun said. "That doesn't look good."

As Yoshi lifted out the large body piece, some of the metal scales fell off. Its lacquer finish was spotted with mildew; the colors of the lacing were faded and moldy.

"This helmet," Yoshi said, lifting it up, "must have been magnificent in its day." Now, though, it was flecked with rust, and one of the metal wings was bent. Yoshi had expected to feel excitement, but the frayed silk and bent metal in his hands

Samurai armor. (*Yuko Shimizu*)

filled him with melancholy. He'd heard it said that the days of the noble samurai were over. Here was the proof: armor dissolving into dust, mildewing into a white powder.

"How could this have happened? How could Hideki have neglected his armor this way? How could it have been overlooked for so long?" Yoshi whispered, feeling in his gut a deep and powerful emptiness. For without the mighty samurai warriors, who would protect them from the barbarians?

As ragged as it all was, Yoshi reverently laid each piece out on the tatami in the right order. First the short kimono and trousers. Shin pads, thigh guards. Next the padded sleeves would be pulled on, and then the chest guard and throat protector. For just a moment he indulged himself, wondering what it would be like to wear this armor, to ride a horse into battle, to wield a flashing katana.

The shoji door slid open abruptly, and the boys looked up to see another young samurai standing there.

Yoshi and Jun went down on their knees as he entered.

"Where is Hideki-san?" the boy demanded. "He is wanted at the assembly."

"Begging your pardon, honorable sir," Yoshi said. "He must have been detained by something very important. Please convey his deepest apologies."

The young samurai nodded at the armor laid out before them. "Is that his armor?" he asked.

"I believe so," Yoshi whispered.

"A disgrace!" the samurai said, then spun on his heel and marched away.

"He said that like it was our fault!" Jun said, once the young man was gone. "Why is everything always our fault?"

Yoshi ignored the question. They had bigger worries. "Where do you suppose Hideki has gone?" he asked. "Should we try to find him? Or what should we do?"

"It's hard to know what to do without someone giving us orders," Jun said.

"You finish this," Yoshi said. "I'll go look for him."

Yoshi walked along the deserted corridor, looking into rooms until he came upon Hideki, wearing his formal haori and hakama, and on his knees. His two swords were laid on the floor before him.

Yoshi entered on his knees, head bowed.

"Yoshi-chan," Hideki whispered. "Please help me." Yoshi glanced up. Hideki's face was wet with tears. "I cannot fight," he said, his voice hoarse. "I do not even *want* to fight!"

It was so quiet, Yoshi could hear the tap of Hideki's tears on the tatami floor.

"I am a coward!" Hideki choked out. "I will disgrace my family and our country. You would be a better warrior than I!"

"Do not say so, my lord," Yoshi whispered.

"Yes, it is true," Hideki said. "I am such a blunderer, it is likely I will be unable even to end my own life."

Yoshi's head jerked up. "No!" he blurted, before he had a chance to compose himself.

"I cannot live with the dishonor, nor can my family. Please help me." Hideki nodded toward the swords on the floor.

"Please do not think of such a thing!" Yoshi pleaded. "I beg you. Just go away for a while. Maybe nothing will come of all this, and people will forget."

"Do you think so?"

"I am sure of it," Yoshi said. "Please, go to the temple. The monks are kind there; they will help you. I will find you some other clothes, so you won't be recognized as easily." He moved toward the door.

"Shh!" Hideki whispered. "Someone is coming!"

Far down the corridor, Yoshi could hear doors sliding open, then shut.

"Quickly, then," Yoshi said. "Take my clothes." He stripped off his rough-spun short kimono and helped Hideki into it. "First chance you get, cover your topknot with a hat!" he added.

"Now you must have my clothes," Hideki insisted.

"No!" Yoshi protested.

The footsteps in the corridor were coming their way.

"Go! Go!" Yoshi whispered.

"Come with me, Yoshi," Hideki begged. "I don't want you to take my punishment."

"No," Yoshi said. "People are looking for you. I will distract them while you get away."

The footsteps drew closer.

"Go—now!" Yoshi urged Hideki out the door.

But what should *he* do? Yoshi wondered. He needed *something* to wear. He'd have to wear Hideki's clothes. He slipped into the wide-legged hakama, rather too long for him, and the haori, also a bit too baggy. He would change into something correct for his station as soon as possible.

Then he noticed Hideki's swords. The shorter wakizashi was there on the floor where it had been placed, and next to it, the katana. *What should be done with them?* Yoshi wondered. He picked up the sword from the floor and held it reverently.

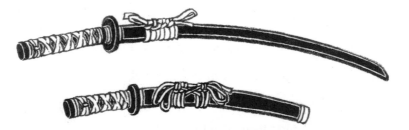

Katana (top); wakizashi (bottom). (*Yuko Shimizu*)

The feel of it startled him; its weight and heft were so different than his bamboo sword. And the blade! The blade seemed to pulse—as if it had its own heartbeat.

Maybe, he thought, *maybe I could take Hideki's place. Maybe I will go to fight the white devils after all.* But with the sound of approaching voices, he gave up the thought. He would have to hide the swords somewhere and find something else to wear, and quickly, before he was discovered in Hideki's clothes.

He stuck his head out of the room, glanced in both directions, and, seeing no one, hurried out across the courtyard.

"Hideki!" a voice behind him shouted. It was Kitsune.

Yoshi froze. Should he run? What should he do? He had promised to distract the others, to help Hideki's flight, so he slowly turned to face Kitsune. The wide-eyed Jun peeked out from behind the big man.

Then Kitsune realized who it was. "On your knees!" he shouted.

Yoshi lowered himself to his knees, respectfully setting the two weapons down as he had so often practiced with his bamboo sword.

At the command, Jun also went down on his knees, and began to tremble.

"What have you done with Hideki?" Kitsune demanded.

Yoshi was silent.

"Speak, worm! Why are you wearing his clothes? And holding his katana? What kind of outrage have you committed?"

What could he say? Yoshi wondered. Nothing. So he remained silent.

"Where is he?"

Again, Yoshi was silent. He knew the longer he could detain Kitsune, the better chance Hideki had of getting away.

"You have committed some kind of horrible act!" Kitsune said.

Behind him Jun trembled so hard, he was like a dog shaking water off itself.

"Why do you laugh?" Kitsune barked at Jun. "What do you find so funny? Control yourself!"

"Excuse me," Yoshi said. "He is not laughing; he is afraid."

Kitsune turned his wrath back on Yoshi. "Why do you speak for him but not for yourself? Tell me what you have done with Hideki—or prepare to die!"

Jun sputtered, his choking sobs indiscernible from gasps of laughter.

"Speak!" Kitsune shouted.

But Yoshi said nothing.

"Then die!" Kitsune said.

With his head still bowed, Yoshi heard the subtle shift of Kitsune's weight, the scrape of his sandal on the dirt. He heard the great, long katana drawn from its scabbard, felt the air move as the sword was raised, sensed the steel blade overhead, so huge it seemed to block out the sun.

He had heard that the earth was as round as a ball, and that it floated in space like a star. It turned, it was said; it spun. How was it he had never felt the earth's movement until now? How was it he had never wondered more about this huge, round earth, even to wonder what lay beyond those hills on the far side of the bay? Now he was seized by longing. Longing to know what else there was on this earth.

The kendo teacher had said a true samurai is ready to die every moment of every day. But Yoshi wasn't a samurai, and he didn't want to die. In fact, he had never wanted to live more than he did at this moment.

These thoughts passed through his mind in an instant, and in the next he tucked his head and rolled forward, knocking Kitsune down. The man sprawled in the dirt, stunned. On the roll, Yoshi picked up Hideki's katana, the way he had seen the kendo teacher do it that very day.

Jun stayed on his knees in the dirt, too petrified to move.

"Run!" Yoshi shouted at him, but Jun just stared at him, open-mouthed.

Kitsune had gathered his wits, risen, and now stood with his katana in his hand. "Then Jun shall take the punishment for both of you," he said, and raised the big sword once more.

5

THE FIGHT

Honorable Kitsune," Yoshi called with as much confidence as he could muster. He intended to have a proper fight with Kitsune, and do as well as he could, but when the fierce-eyed samurai turned, Yoshi forgot all his practice. He closed his eyes and took a wild swing with Hideki's sword. He felt the blade sweeping through the air and slicing through something—he hoped it wasn't flesh— but when he opened his eyes, he saw blood.

Kitsune's hand went to his face, where a bloody gash had opened his cheek. The startled man looked at the blood on his hand and turned his eyes on Yoshi.

"You!" Spit sprayed from Kitsune's mouth. "Your life is not worth *this*." He kicked dust from the ground.

Yoshi knew it, and in quick succession he dropped the katana, grabbed Jun's arm, yanked him to his feet, and ran, half-dragging the boy behind him.

The two boys scampered up and over the garden wall, across the bridge, and down the dirt road, finally veering onto a path that cut deep into the forest.

"I'll find you!" Kitsune's voice echoed through the forest. "I'll follow you and you will be punished!"

"Wouldn't you think he'd be more worried about the barbarians than about two peasants like us?" Jun panted.

Yoshi didn't answer. He was running too hard to say anything, pushed on by the thudding of footsteps behind them. He yanked Jun behind a bunch of thickly clustered hydrangea bushes, and the two boys crouched there, breathing hard.

"Do you think it's true what they say about Kitsune?" Jun whispered. "That a fox spirit got into him and he can turn into one of them?"

"No, that can't be true," Yoshi whispered back. "Listen to him crashing around. And the way he walks? *Thud thud thud.* If he were really a fox, he would step more softly."

"I'll find you dogs!" Kitsune's voice cut through the hydrangeas the way his sword sliced off the big, globe-like flowers. "You should know to be obedient and loyal to the family who took you in, who looked after you!"

"He's talking about you," Jun whispered.

"Shh!" Yoshi hushed him. He knew he owed loyalty to the family who had kept him on as a servant after his mother had died, but did that loyalty extend even to having his head lopped off? "Our whole lives long, we are as good as invisible," he whispered. "Nobody seems to see us. Nobody *wants* to see us. Why is it that when we *need* to be invisible, then no such luck?"

"I'm working on it," Jun whispered. "That is, becoming invisible. I've been practicing." His eyes gleamed in the flickering green light.

"You'd better make yourself invisible *now!*" Yoshi whispered as the crashing sounds drew nearer.

Jun squeezed his eyes shut, while Yoshi watched the flashing blade cleanly slice through the bushes not far from where they crouched. The blossoms, each as big as a child's head, toppled from the stalks.

"Did it work?" Jun whispered.

Yoshi glanced at him. "No," he said. He turned his attention back to the movement of the bushes. After a moment, he said, "Kitsune has moved away. But he may come back. We'd better get out of here."

The boys climbed out of the bushes and ran, Yoshi holding up his too-long trouser legs so he wouldn't trip. They turned first onto this path, then that, through forests of pine and cypress. Broadsheets attached to the trees fluttered in the wind. Even a quick glance was enough to see they were printed with an edict forbidding anyone to go near the Black Ships.

People passed the boys, climbing the hills, moving away

from the coast. Pattering along the trails, they made a sound as if the forest were whispering sutras. Temple bells tolled and tolled, endlessly tolling.

"Where did you learn how to do that, anyway?" Jun panted. "Knocking Kitsune down and taking the sword, I mean."

"The kendo master just taught us that move today," Yoshi said.

"Us?"

"Well," Yoshi said, "you were napping."

"Yoshi," Jun panted as they jogged along the path, "our lives are not worth a copper penny now. If word of Hideki's cowardice were to get out . . ." He stopped. "He ran away, didn't he?"

Yoshi didn't answer.

"You traded clothes with him and he ran."

Again, Yoshi said nothing.

"Well," Jun said, "Kitsune will figure it out, and let's just say, the family would not want that piece of information known. They will look all over in the village, in the forest, at the temple. Nowhere is safe! Kitsune will find us and kill us for sure! Where can we go?"

And then, suddenly, Yoshi knew where they could go. "Where is the one place he won't look for us?" Yoshi said. "Where is the one place he will assume we will never go?"

Jun turned to Yoshi, his eyes gleaming in the fading light.

"But it is forbidden to go there!" he whispered. "You can't be serious!"

"Yes," Yoshi said, "I am." The thought of it made him shiver a little with fright. Or was it excitement?

6

THE WATERFRONT, TOWN OF URAGA

The waterfront had been deserted by the usual crowd of ferryboat men, travelers, and fishermen and was instead a chaotic scene of armed samurai police and soldiers who had been sent to protect the country. None of them noticed the two dusty and ragged boys who kept to the lengthening shadows of the pines.

It was a warm, humid evening. The scent of the sea lay heavy in the air, and the smoke of sentry fires and gunpowder hung like mist over the water. There was something else, too, Yoshi thought. Maybe the smell of the ships, carrying the scent of far-off places, frightening places, places he couldn't even imagine.

In the gathering darkness, the Black Ships were almost invisible. Still, Yoshi could sense them there, lurking in the bay like malevolent dragons. The air of mystery surrounding them was almost unbearable. Both boys shivered a little, despite the warmth of the evening.

"At least we're safe," Yoshi said, settling down in a spot among the trees.

"Maybe from Kitsune," Jun said. "I'm not so sure we're safe from *them*! Do you think they can see us?"

"No. How?" Yoshi said.

"It is said the hairy ones can see in the dark," Jun said. "Like cats."

"They are too far away. We can't see them; they can't see us." Yoshi stared at the vague black shapes.

Without taking his eyes off the ships, Jun sat down next to him.

"Do you ever wish you could sail far away out into the ocean?" Yoshi asked.

"No!" Jun said. "Why would I want to do that? There is nothing good there. Barbarians. Monsters. The sea priest who lures fishermen to their deaths. Would *you* want to go there?"

Yoshi lay back. "I don't know. I'm too tired to think," he said, but his nerves buzzed.

"How will we ever sleep?" Jun said. "I'm so hungry!"

"Oh!" Yoshi sat up, remembering the rice ball tucked into the fold of his sleeve. Ah, but Hideki was now wearing that garment. Well, Hideki would probably have gotten hungry, too, he supposed.

How, Yoshi wondered, had he managed to bungle things so badly? Now he was hungry, without a job; his life wasn't worth a copper penny; and the barbarians were about to invade the country. There was no use feeling sorry for himself. He had wished for things to change, he reminded himself, and they had.

Jun was already snoring when Yoshi lay back again and stared up into the darkness. The sky was like a deep, vast ocean, dotted with shimmering islands. What would it be like to be up there, steering a boat from one bright star to the next? The world where these ships had come from, Yoshi wondered— what was it like? Had they come from some island as bright as a star?

Yoshi fell asleep imagining swimming from star to star, though he didn't know how to swim very well. But in his dream he struck off with bold strokes across a black ocean, aiming for the brightest star he could see.

7

THE COMET

Early morning hours of July 9, 1853

An interesting meteorological phenomenon was observed in the course
of the night . . . a remarkable meteor seen from midnight until four
o'clock in the morning.

—M. C. Perry, *Narrative of the Expedition*
to the China Seas and Japan, 1852–1854

Jack woke to a potent stench and an eerie bluish light
pouring through the round glass deadlight in the decking
directly above his hammock. The blue light was unfamiliar.
The stink, however, he immediately identified: Toley's reeking
boots and filthy stockings, which had once again been tossed
into Willis's hammock, right next to his own. The items might
as well have been put in Jack's berth, so closely together were
the hammocks slung.

He considered picking up the boots and dropping them on
Toley's sleeping form, but he thought better of it. Willis would

probably be blamed and earn a sneaky punch in the gut from Toley when nobody was looking. Jack knew that was how the older boy kept the younger one in line. Why else would Willis go along with him, except that Toley was just enough older, just enough bigger, and just enough wilier to win every time.

Well, Jack thought as he climbed the companionway ladder, he didn't suppose there was much he could do about it.

When he emerged on the upper deck, he was greeted by an unearthly light that bathed everything in its strange glow: Every spar and sail and each one of the four ships' hulls shimmered in the same blue light that cast a metallic sheen upon the water of the bay.

Some of his shipmates stood at the bulwark, looking at two very different spectacles. Overhead, a strangely bright blue sphere moved slowly across the sky, trailing behind it a red tail, from which it seemed sparks flew, while below, all along the hillsides, glimmered hundreds of bonfires.

"Beacon fires," he heard a sailor say. "The smaller ones are sentry fires, I think."

Every hamlet and village up and down the hills and all along the coast was illuminated by hundreds of such fires, while the flickering of torches moving from place to place looked like swarms of fireflies against the dark hills.

Jack stared at the sight, and only when he heard voices did

he realize that Commodore Perry himself was standing nearby, surveying the scene, with the purser and the first lieutenant.

"We should construe this as a favorable omen," the commodore said, gazing up at the comet, "that our mission shall succeed without resort to bloodshed." He held a small telescope to his eye, looked at the hills for a good while, and sniffed. "A few unfinished forts, and I warrant only a handful of them with cannon, and those of no great caliber. The Japanese probably have not calculated on the exactness of view afforded by a Dolland's telescope or, for that matter, a French opera glass." He collapsed the telescope, turned, and caught sight of Jack.

Jack saluted and tried to back away before he was scolded, but the commodore fixed his gaze on him as if he were the bull's-eye on a target.

"What's your name, son?" the commodore asked.

"Jack Sullivan, sir. Cabin boy, and," Jack quickly added, "powder monkey."

"We are hopeful that your services will not be needed in that role," the commodore said.

"Aye, sir," Jack replied.

"How old are you?"

Jack cleared his throat and tried to get his voice to sound a little deeper. "Thirteen, sir," he said.

The commodore turned to the lieutenant and said, "This boy and one other of the same height should be in the procession when—and if—we deliver the president's letter to the mikado. We'll have them carry the boxes with the letters."

Once the commodore had swept off, the lieutenant pursed his lips and glowered down at Jack, who knew what the officer was thinking: This troublemaker? Jack imagined the lieutenant tallying up his misdeeds: inattentiveness to the door of the chicken coop, tangled lines, overturned slush buckets, and—

"What happened to your buttons?" the lieutenant asked.

Jack glanced down at his jacket. Sure enough, two of his buttons were missing. Probably the earlier struggle with the chicken was responsible. He stammered but couldn't quite get anything intelligible out.

"See to it that you've replaced those and are looking ship-shape before going ashore."

"Aye, aye, sir!" Jack said.

"There will be a thorough briefing before the landing," the lieutenant went on, "but one thing you should know is that I will not stand for any show of obsequiousness. Not on the deck of an American man-of-war, not under the flag of the United States. Do you understand?"

"Aye, aye, sir," Jack repeated.

The lieutenant stalked off, and Jack turned to see Griggs

leaning against the bulwark not far off. "What was he talking about?" Jack asked.

"Ah," Griggs said, pushing himself off the rail. "He wants none o' that scrapin' one's forehead on the ground what these folk are 'customed to do. He wants none such obsqueakiness from his crew."

Jack made a mental note to avoid any show of that—what Griggs said—and then he kicked up his heels. He would be among the first to go ashore in the fabled land of Japan!

8

THE STEAMING TEAPOT

BOOM!

Yoshi woke to the roar of a cannon. He sat bolt upright. And again: *BOOM! BOOM!* He cowered at the sound of the explosions. Had the war started while he and Jun had been sleeping?

BOOM!

Jun sat up next to him, his mouth wide open, his eyes blinking rapidly. "What just happened?" he asked. "What's going on?"

"It was the barbarian cannon that woke us." Yoshi pointed at the smoke hanging over the water.

"Are we at war?" Jun asked.

Yoshi glanced at the soldiers and workers near the waterfront, now unfolding themselves from their crouching positions or appearing from behind trees.

"Just a morning salute!" an official called out. "Some kind of barbarian custom. Not an attack. Go back to your stations."

"Not an attack," Yoshi whispered, taking a deep breath.

Samurai gather to defend the homeland against the foreign invasion.
(*Toshu Shogetsu*)

"Look at all those warriors!" Jun said. "Pikemen, cavalry-men armed with muskets, mounted samurai . . . And what are those workers doing with those baskets?"

"It looks like they're building an earthen wall," Yoshi answered. He looked beyond the activity to the big ships in the bay. Now, in the daylight, he could really see them lurking there, each one anchored broadside to the shore. That was so they could aim their cannons directly at the village, he'd overheard a soldier say. He seethed with anger at the affront. "How dare they defile the waters of Edo Bay and threaten the Sacred Land of the Rising Sun," he said.

"How dare they defy the laws of our country forbidding all barbarians to come near," Jun agreed.

"Don't you wish we were samurai, so we could fight and repel the white devils?" Yoshi asked Jun.

"I think we should get out of here," Jun said.

"Wait," Yoshi said. "Look at those boats approaching the Black Ships. What are they doing?" Some were guard boats stuffed with Japanese soldiers who held up a big banner with strange lines and markings on it. "I think the sign says something in their language, maybe."

"It doesn't look like language," Jun said. "It looks more like ink spatters. Like someone trying to get ink off a brush."

"What are the men in those other boats doing?" Yoshi

asked. He pointed to boats crowded with men whose heads bobbed up and down like birds drinking from a puddle.

"It looks like they're writing . . . or drawing," Jun said.

"Ah!" Yoshi exclaimed. "They are sketching! They are making drawings of the barbarians. Wouldn't that be something to see?"

"Yoshitaro," Jun said, "we should get out of here before something terrible happens."

"Let's just wait until the artists get back. Maybe we can see what the hairy ones look like."

"I'll tell you what they look like," Jun said. "They are hairy. Now, let's go!"

"Don't you want to see?" Yoshi asked. "Do they have horns? And fangs? And tails?"

"No, I don't want to see," Jun said. "I'm going to go to my aunt and uncle's house in the country. You can come, too. I know you don't have anywhere to go. I'm sure they'll take you in. Come on!"

Yoshi looked toward the shore where one of the artists' boats was now landing.

Jun tugged on Yoshi's sleeve. "Please!"

Yoshi knew it made sense to follow Jun. He glanced back at the forested hills. He looked at the water of the bay, sparkling in the summer sun. "Be fluid like water," he remembered the kendo teacher saying. "Water can fill a vessel of any shape and is able to make itself into a single drop or a vast ocean." He turned back to Jun. "You go," he said. "I'm going to stay."

As soon as Jun was gone, Yoshi hurried to the waterfront.

"Honorable sir," he said, bowing to one of the artists standing on the shore, "may I see your pictures?" He couldn't believe how bold he was being. It was as if basic etiquette had been thrown out the window because of all the things that had happened.

"In due time, in due time," said the artist. "You'll have an opportunity to purchase a picture of the foreign devils."

"I have no money," Yoshi said, hanging his head, but then he quickly added, "You must be quite brave, to row out so close to the barbarians."

"No, no!" the man said. "Not at all. I was too busy to be afraid. But *you* must be quite brave, since here you are, near the barbarian ships, while others have run away."

"Not brave," Yoshi confessed. "Just stupid!"

The old artist laughed, and for the first time since all this had happened, Yoshi laughed, too. "What did the hairy ones look like?" he asked. "Are they really as white as porcelain? Could you smell them? People say they stink because they eat flesh."

"I wasn't close enough to smell them," the artist said. "But their ships smell like gunpowder!"

Yoshi took a furtive glance at the rolls of rice paper the man carried, but as they were all rolled up, he couldn't make out any of the images.

"You're a curious boy, aren't you, little samurai?" the artist asked, looking him up and down.

"Oh!" Yoshi exclaimed. "I am not really bushi. That is . . . these are not my clothes."

The man raised an eyebrow. "Well, no need to explain. These are desperate times. So you are curious and you are not afraid. And you are honest, too!"

Yoshi bowed, saying, "It seems I possess nothing at all *except* honesty."

"Then, my boy," the artist said, "you possess the most important thing, for as we know, 'The gods dwell in the heads of the honest.' Now, are you hungry?"

Yoshi nodded.

"Here's a chance for you to earn a few coins for yourself, and with them you can buy whatever you'd like to eat."

Again Yoshi bowed.

"My name is Ozawa. There is a shop in Edo where they know my name and will make prints of these images right away. I want you to take these there."

"In . . . Edo?" Yoshi could barely bring himself to say the word. Edo was the biggest city in all of Japan. There dwelled the shogun, the great lords, and the Bakufu, the ruling body of all of Japan!

"Here is a travel permit. And here is money for the ferry, for the prints, and to get something to eat. Oh!" The artist pressed another coin into Yoshi's palm. "Get me some of those buns filled with sweetened bean paste that they sell near the Nihon Bridge. You know your way around Edo, don't you?"

Yoshi shook his head.

"I shall draw you a map, then," Ozawa said.

Yoshi recoiled. "I don't know if I am allowed to have a map . . . ," he murmured.

"Yes," Ozawa said. "So many things are forbidden now: calendars, most new books—the Bakufu believes we have enough books already—and pictures of barbarians, and . . ." He rattled off the list of pictures that were forbidden while he continued drawing.

When he was finished, he handed Yoshi the paper and said, "See? This is just a picture of an ordinary samurai's face. All you need to know is that his forehead is the shogun's castle, his topknot is the Yoshiwara—no need for you to go there. The mouth is the mouth of the Sumida River, and the creases in the face are all the many canals. See these two eyes? Yes, here in the very center of the right eye is the engraver's shop. You shouldn't have any trouble finding it. It lies in the shadow of the samurai's forehead, by which I mean the—"

"Shogun's castle," Yoshi finished.

"Tell them Ozawa sent you," the artist went on. "And then come right back—after stopping for buns, of course—right here"—he pointed to the samurai's nostril—"and there will be more money for you to earn, because once I get the prints"—Ozawa thumped the rolled-up papers against his hand—"I'll need an enterprising assistant to sell them for me."

"Sell them?" Yoshi looked around at the waterfront, deserted except for the soldiers and workers building earthen fortifications. "To whom?"

"Don't you worry," the artist said. "This place will soon be jammed with curiosity seekers."

"Really?" Yoshi wondered aloud. "But the edict says that everyone is to stay away from the Black Ships."

The artist waved his hand dismissively. "Yes, edicts and more edicts. People will get over their fear and want to see—just as you did. And what do you suppose? The Bakufu will pay good money to see these pictures. Why? Because they want to know about these American ships. How many cannon? What size? What other weapons do they have? These are the things the shogun's councillors want to know. When they see these pictures"—here Ozawa held up one of a steamship with its

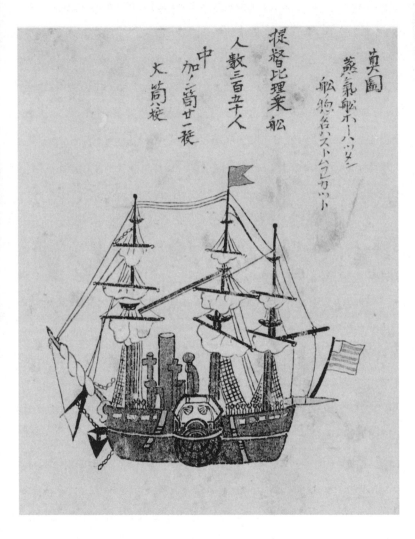

Perry's flagship, as drawn by an anonymous Japanese artist. The commentary reads: "Crew of 350. Twenty-one medium cannon, 8 large cannon."

cannon barrels sticking out of the gun ports—"oh, yes, little samurai, things are about to change," he said. "In ways we cannot imagine."

Things had already changed for Yoshi. He had a new job with a new master. How much more different could things be?

Ozawa broke into song. "What a joke: the steaming teapot fixed by America—" he sang. "Just four cups, and we cannot sleep at night!" He turned to Yoshi. "Off you go!" he urged, and Yoshi ran off to the waterfront to find a ferryboat.

Riding on the ferry, Yoshi tried to decipher what Ozawa's steaming teapot song meant. Perhaps it had to do with the steamships. "Just four cups" referred to the four ships that steamed into the air like hot teapots. And "we cannot sleep at night"? Maybe fear of the ships took away sleep, the way strong tea sometimes did. But to lose sleep because of only four cups of tea? Maybe the song was saying that people were getting all worked up over nothing.

By the looks of things, people were surely getting worked up. The countryside was in a frenzy. Yoshi watched multitudes of people struggling up steep hillsides carrying their belongings. The boat in which he rode, like hundreds of others plying the bay, was crowded with mothers and children being sent to stay with distant relatives.

And while ordinary people were fleeing the nearby villages, soldiers and warriors were flooding toward the town of Uraga.

Yoshi could feel the other passengers staring at him. It was his clothes, he knew. He was likely to get into trouble wearing them. There was only one thing to do: At the first opportunity, he would sell them and get himself proper clothing. Meanwhile, he paid a penny for a dome-like straw hat—too big for him, so it covered a large part of his face. This was on purpose. The last thing he needed right now was to be recognized by Kitsune.

9

EDO

Edo! The biggest of all Japanese cities! The home of the shogun. Here was where all the great lords spent at least part of every year. Here was where a million people lived and worked . . . and worried, it looked like to Yoshi.

The streets were crowded with people hurrying this way and that. Here a mother rushed along with children in her arms, there a man carried his elderly mother on his back, everyone looking for a safe place to hide family and belongings.

Yoshi moved along, trying to stay out from under the hooves of the warhorses and out of the way of tramping soldiers. Everywhere, he heard the clang of metal on metal: helmets being straightened and swords sharpened. Lines of servants holding tattered armor formed outside the tailors' shops. Yoshi thought of the boom of the cannon, its fire and smoke, and wondered if that armor, against those guns, offered any better protection than wearing a suit of rice paper.

This made him remember his own incorrect clothing,

A Japanese print shop. (*Ando Hiroshige*)

and he ducked into a small shop on a side street. The shopkeeper rubbed the fabric between his fingers and, almost purring, offered what Yoshi thought must be a fair price for the haori and hakama. The shopkeeper even gave him a short kimono and leggings to wear.

Wearing more proper attire, Yoshi reentered the street and studied Ozawa's map. He didn't need it to find the shogun's palace. As he drew closer, he could see the many buildings of the castle grounds. Beyond the moats, the castle's many gateways and massive doors, he knew, were all guarded by armed sentries and soldiers. The white walls of the castle keep rose and rose, like one castle balanced on another, so high it made him dizzy to look up. Thankfully, he was not required to go there.

In the shadow of the castle, he found the engraver's shop. The inside was cluttered with pots of ink, colored paint, stacks of rice paper, rags, and all kinds of tools and brushes, and it smelled pleasantly of ink and wood shavings. Workers busy at their tasks barely glanced up as he was shown into the shop.

A man greeted him, and Yoshi presented the ink drawings, whispering the name of Ozawa.

"Ah, yes," the engraver said. "Tell your master we will take care of it. The prints will be sent to him when they are finished."

"Will you know where to find him?" Yoshi asked.

"Wherever the barbarians are," the man said, "is where Ozawa will be found."

Bowing, Yoshi backed out the door.

He then went straight to the shop that sold the buns and bought several for Ozawa and two for himself. He sat down and ate his on the spot, savoring the delicious burst of sweetened bean paste in his mouth. It was so good! Next he bought himself a meal of grilled fish and eggplant in miso paste. He could have kept eating all day. He thought of the money he had gotten for Hideki's clothes. He could spend some of that for more food, he supposed. *No*, he thought, *I am going to save it for Hideki, since I can't give him back his clothes.*

Next he found a shrine where he could offer a prayer. He rang the bell, clapped to get the attention of the gods, and dropped a small coin into the waiting pot. He knew he should be praying, as others were, for kamikaze—the divine wind— to come and blow the invaders away, but secretly he prayed that when the barbarians came warring, he would be given a sword, in order that he might help fight them.

10

BRUSH VERSUS SWORD

Upon his return to Uraga, Yoshi was able to find Ozawa with little difficulty. He spotted him near the waterfront, his round, bald head with its ring of white hair bent over his work. As Yoshi waited for Ozawa to finish, he began to feel that something about the artist seemed familiar. He reminded Yoshi of someone. Then he knew: It was the sword master! Was it how he held the brush? How he seemed so comfortable with it—as if it were an extension of his arm? Was it how he used his brush the way the sword master used his katana—as if they were one being? How he made confident sweeping movements with it? Or his total concentration while he worked?

Perhaps sensing Yoshi standing nearby, Ozawa said, "Would you like to draw something?"

"Oh, I'm not good at it," Yoshi said.

"I didn't ask if you were good, only if you'd like to try." Ozawa held out brush and paper. "Here, try!"

"Really? Me?"

The artist glanced around him and said, "I don't see anyone else standing there."

Using the artist's offered brush and inkstone, Yoshi carefully painted a horse.

"Not terrible!" Ozawa said. He made a few suggestions for improvement, and Yoshi tried again. The next picture was better, and the next even better than that. "Better and better!" Ozawa commented, looking over Yoshi's shoulder. "Perhaps you have talent!"

Yoshi thought perhaps he *would* like drawing.

While Yoshi practiced, Ozawa munched on the bean paste buns and gave Yoshi pointers. Then he talked about how Japanese officials had been received on one of the big ships, where they had asked the barbarians to leave. As anyone could see just by looking, the ships hadn't gone anywhere. The red-hairs had then been asked to move their ships to Nagasaki. They hadn't. Instead, they had threatened to take their ships to Edo—in which case, they were told, the Japanese officials who had allowed such a thing would be forced to slice open their own bellies by committing seppuku.

Although no one dared say any of these things aloud, it was whispered that the hairy ones could—and would—do anything they wanted to. It was whispered even more quietly that the shogun seemed unable to stop them.

"Our warriors' swords will stop them," Yoshi said, fervently hoping it was true.

"I think it's more likely that *this* will stop them," Ozawa said, holding up a paintbrush, "than swords."

"How can that be?" Yoshi said. He looked up from his drawing. He was trying to draw a picture of a katana with a fancy hilt.

"A brush can cut deeper than a sword, and, unlike a sword, it can also heal. And, really"—Ozawa examined his brush as if it were a precious thing—"the brush is more powerful than a sword. It speaks truth when truth cannot be spoken any other way." He nodded at Yoshi's drawing. "What can you say for your sword? Which would you pick, given a choice? Brush or sword?"

Yoshi didn't need to think about it. "A sword!" he said, holding up his finished drawing. "A sword can slash and cut. You can hear it sing as it slices the air. It makes real work for your muscles to do—not just your brain. Can a brush be so sharp that it can cut a flower petal floating down a river? No. Therefore, a sword is preferable."

"Well, you have a certain logic," Ozawa said. "And you argue well. But can a sword transport you to other places, show you things you've never seen or even thought of before? Can a sword make magic?"

"Magic?"

"Certainly you've heard the story of the boy who was so

crazy about drawing that he neglected his religious studies?" The artist's voice changed to storytelling mode, and Yoshi set down his brush to listen. "The abbot became so angry with the youngster that he tied him to a post to prevent him from drawing. There the lad stood all the day long, with his arms tied to the post. At last the abbot returned, ready to release the young fellow. But as he reached for the ropes, what should he see but rats running underfoot, poised to bite the youngster's bare feet! Only after he had untied the boy did the abbot see that the rats were only *drawings* the poor child had made in the dust, with his toe for a brush and his tears for ink."

"No!" Yoshi exclaimed.

"Yes!" the artist said. "Of course, seeing his talent, the abbot regretted his harsh punishment and from then on let the boy draw all he wanted. That boy grew up to be Sesshu Toyo, one of our greatest artists."

"That couldn't really happen, though," Yoshi said.

"Well, perhaps you are right," Ozawa offered. "Some say that what really happened is that the rats that Toyo drew gnawed through his ropes and freed him."

"That is also too far-fetched to believe," Yoshi insisted.

"How much do we fail to imagine is possible just because it does not *seem* possible?" Ozawa said. "Perhaps the impossible is just exactly what we should try to imagine." He looked out at the ships. "Who would have imagined a ship that moves without sails? Had you?"

Yoshi shook his head.

"Someone did," Ozawa said. "And there they are." He picked up the brush, dipped it in the wet ink, pressed down, turned it, pressed down again. "The era of the sword will end, perhaps soon." He glanced at the ships. "Their guns have made the sword obsolete already." Yoshi looked out over the water at the Black Ships. Still anchored broadside to the bay, they looked solid and immovable. They looked like they had every intention of staying there, and that they would stay as long as they felt like it.

"The only thing that everyone seems to agree upon is that to fight the foreigners is to fight to the death," Ozawa said. "It seems that although the barbarians won't back down on our demand to leave the country, neither do they intend to start the fight. You can see for yourself." He pointed the tip of his brush at the ships. "They simply stay!"

Yoshi burned with anger at those who would defy the laws of his land. Who did they think they were? The Sacred Land of the Rising Sun would not stand for this affront! The mighty samurai warriors would rise against the barbarians and send them away!

He hoped.

11

THE SALESMAN

Towels! Scrolls! Fans!" Yoshi shouted from his perch on an overturned bucket. He unrolled a scroll so his audience could see the colored print. "Images of the hairy ones! See their bulbous noses—big and bumpy as ginger roots! See their frightening, icicle-colored eyes and their hairy, hairy faces! Prepare to be astounded! You will hardly believe what you see!"

Every day, Yoshi's countrymen had become less fearful and more curious, and every day the crowd at the waterfront grew larger. The audience gasped, clucked, oohed, retrieved money from sleeves or pouches, and paid for a keepsake fan or scroll or towel. Soon his pouch bulged with coins. It wasn't strictly *his* money; still, it gave him a feeling of—well, he didn't know what it was, for he'd never felt it before, but it was a good feeling, in any case.

Not long after, Ozawa approached while Yoshi was counting out coins and said, "I have some news! The Americans are going to come ashore."

Yoshi raised his head. "Really?" he asked. His stomach buzzed and fluttered as if filled with crowds of dragonflies.

"His High and Mighty Mysteriousness, the American mikado, is going to deliver a letter from the king of America," Ozawa crowed. "So it is said."

"When?"

"Soon." Ozawa smiled. "And we'll be allowed to get close to the procession to make sketches."

"We?"

"Yes," Ozawa said. "We. Unless you are too afraid?"

"I'm not afraid!" Yoshi answered, perhaps not being entirely truthful.

"Good," Ozawa said. "Because I am going to need my assistant."

12

THE LETTER FROM THE PRESIDENT

The marines led the way, and the sailors following, the Commodore was duly escorted up the beach. . . . Two boys, dressed for the ceremony, preceded the Commodore, bearing in an envelope of scarlet cloth the boxes which contained his credentials and the President's letter.

—M. C. Perry, *Narrative of the Expedition to the China Seas and Japan, 1852–1854*

Jack knew he was marching, but he almost felt as if he were floating, he was so excited. In fact, he was so excited, or maybe so nervous, that he'd leaped out of the boat a little early, and splashed into water up to his knees.

The Americans' procession. (artist unknown)

"Are you trying to be the first to touch Japanese soil?" joked Smith, one of the sailors. "Too late, for Captain Buchanan has taken that honor."

It was lucky the ships' bands were playing, because the music covered the sounds of his wet shoes squish-squishing and his heart hammering away. He knew he should keep a serious demeanor—eyes straight ahead, focus forward—but there was so much to look at!

The Americans' procession, he thought, was quite impressive. The commodore had seen to that. A company of one hundred marines and a company of that many sailors headed the parade. Two of the biggest and burliest sailors carried the flag and pennant, and two black crewmen, both very tall, had been selected to march alongside Commodore Perry.

Jack and another boy walked just ahead of the commodore, each carrying a large scarlet cloth envelope containing a rosewood box. Within the boxes were letters to the mikado: one from the president of the United States and one from the commodore.

Although the Americans were strong in number—probably three hundred souls in all—that was nothing compared to the Japanese presence. Thousands upon thousands of Japanese warriors, some on foot and some mounted, some carrying pikes and some longbows and feathered arrows crowded the area. Jack had never seen so many swords. In addition to the warriors, at least another thousand Japanese onlookers stood silently and politely behind the barricades.

Sketch artists from the ships, as well as a row of Japanese artists, were situated along the parade route, drawing away. Jack longed to get a look at the sketches to see how the Americans were being depicted. As he passed by the artists, he tried to look as regal, serious, handsome, and *tall* as he possibly could in his uniform, with every single button in place—sewn on with great care by Jack Sullivan himself.

Just as he was thinking proudly of his newfound sewing skill, something pinged into the gravel at his feet. Glancing down, he saw that it was a button. Apparently he hadn't done as good a job stitching them on as he'd thought. Without getting out of step, he scooped up the button. When he stood, his eye snagged the eyes of a Japanese boy about his own age: same height, same size, but in every other way completely and utterly different. He was darker, his hair shiny and black, his nose small, and his eyes almond shaped. His eyes! So dark—almost black—and for a moment Jack's own eyes were locked with them.

The boy, though small, looked strong, like he might have a good pitching arm. But what was Jack thinking? This boy

The American expedition's artist, William Heine, sketching, as portrayed by an anonymous Japanese artist.

wouldn't even *know* about baseball! The thought made him smile.

The boy smiled back. He was just a kid! Jack thought. They might even be friends, if only the boy wasn't a heathen.

Yoshi glanced up just in time to see a boy looking at him, a boy about his age, and the same height, but in every other way completely and utterly different. The boy had strange, extreme features: a sharp nose, a sharp chin, and pale skin—except for a smattering of darker spots that ran up and over his nose. And his hair! It was so red, yet it still seemed as if the color had been rinsed out of it. His eyes, too, were so pale as to be almost translucent. Was the boy sick? Maybe sick with some contagious barbarian disease! Except that his cheeks wore a blush of health, or maybe excitement.

The boy gave Yoshi a crooked smile. It looked like there could be fun—and trouble—in that smile. And Yoshi couldn't help but smile back. He's just a boy, Yoshi thought. They might even have been friends, if only the boy wasn't a barbarian.

He watched as the procession moved on, and the boy, along with the dignitaries, entered the treaty house.

"Now is the time to sell more of the prints," Ozawa told him. "The crowd will be hungry for them. Go!"

Yoshi snatched up the bundle of fans and scrolls and

umbrellas that had been printed with images of the outsiders and their Black Ships. "See the barbarians here!" he called out. "See their faces—hairy as snow monkeys! With noses as big and bulbous as ginger roots. And their spooky blue eyes! See their comical and impractical style of dressing! Remember this historic moment with a one-of-a-kind keepsake."

People crushed in on all sides, reaching out with money for the prints, and soon Yoshi's pouch was heavy with coins. But he and Ozawa had planned well and brought plenty of towels and fans and umbrellas, and Yoshi continued to move along.

"Get your keepsake of the bar—" he began again, when through the crowd his eye caught a familiar face, a familiar face with an ugly-looking wound along one side.

How could he have let down his guard? Of course representatives from Hideki's family were bound to be here! And of course that meant the head of bodyguards, Kitsune, would accompany them.

Now Kitsune stood merely a few feet from Yoshi, separated only by a wall of customers. Yoshi's heart raced. He swallowed the last part of the word "—barians," turned, and ran.

13

INSIDE THE TREATY HOUSE

Jack tried not to move, because his wet shoes squeaked if he did, and an air of solemnity permeated the inside of the pavilion. The Japanese officials, the commodore, and the most senior officers were seated on a raised platform. Jack, along with other lesser dignitaries, was given a seat on the lower level.

The Japanese officials looked gloomy and downcast, Jack thought. Their expressions seemed to say that this was great fun for the Americans and anything but fun for them.

There was a lot of bowing and a tedious amount of translating. It seemed to Jack as if the English was being translated first into Dutch and then into Japanese and from Japanese to Dutch and from Dutch to English. Wouldn't this be simpler if they cut out the Dutch middleman? Or was there not one soul in all of Japan who could speak English?

Everyone was served a greenish tea that Jack thought tasted like grass. In fact, if he closed his eyes, the whole place smelled like the hayloft back at the farm, loaded with fresh-cut hay. Probably because of the woven-grass mats that covered the floor.

The commodore beckoned to the two boys to bring forth the boxes, and Jack stepped forward, hoping that he wasn't leaving a wet trail behind him. He presented his box to one of the black crewmen who came forward to receive them. The rosewood box was opened, and within it was another box of pure gold. Within that box was the president's letter, bound in blue silk velvet and sealed by cords of gold and silk with golden tassels. Both letters were taken out and laid upon the lid of the Japanese box placed to receive them. All this happened in perfect silence.

Jack knew that the two letters were from the president of the United States and the commodore to the emperor of Japan. He even knew a bit about what was in the letters: requests for trade, for open ports where American ships might stop for provisions, water, coal, and the like. Protestations of friendship. And a demand that shipwrecked American sailors be treated hospitably.

But as more tedious translation took place, Jack began to get itchy, like he did at home when his family went to church. He'd glance at the big oak that stood outside the church window and wish he was in its leafy branches.

Just outside the treaty house was a camellia tree, covered with flowers, and practically as big as the oak at home. He'd like to climb that tree, he thought. He'd like to race through those fields out there—to really run—something he hadn't done since he'd gone aboard the *Susquehanna* seven months earlier. He wanted to climb a tree, feel moss and earth under his feet, touch grass, smell dirt.

So, he thought, *could we add just one more request to the president's letter? Could it also request that one Jack Sullivan be allowed to roam about in your fields and forests? Climb your trees? Cast a line and try for fish in your streams?*

At last, the interminable interview was over, and the commodore said he looked forward to a reply from the mikado and would be back in one year. And next time, the commodore made a point to say, he would be bringing more ships.

14

THE CHASE

Yoshi darted through the crowd, trying to stay low. Even over all the noise and chaos, he sensed Kitsune's hard breathing behind him.

"Stop that rascal!" Kitsune shouted. "Catch that little thief!"

Yoshi halted abruptly, spun around, and protested, "I may be a lot of things, but I am not, nor will I ever be, a thief!" Then he turned and bolted into the throng.

Since most of the spectators had bowed their heads to the honorable samurai, no one had seen where the "rascal" had gone.

People were on their way back to their homes and villages on foot or by the many ferryboats that lined the waterfront for the occasion. If he could time it right, Yoshi thought, he might be able to escape Kitsune. He made a final dash through the crowds, heading for the bay.

There was the shore, and there, just pulling away from it, a ferry. Yoshi put on a burst of speed, raced down to the water's edge, and flung himself onto the departing boat.

Kitsune appeared at the water's edge, red-faced and shouting: "Bring that little troublemaker back here at once!"

A Japanese ferry. (*Ando Hiroshige*)

The boatman looked at Yoshi; he looked back at the fierce-looking samurai. Anybody could see he'd be in trouble no matter what he did. His solution was to pluck Yoshi up by the collar of his tunic and toss him overboard.

The last thing Yoshi heard before his head went underwater was the laughter of the passengers.

The cold water quickly seeped through his clothes. Never mind his clothes! What about the prints and fans? The towels and umbrellas? They were ruined!

Down he went, and he only managed to get his head above water with a lot of thrashing and kicking. He took a big gulp of air and noticed scrolls and fans floating or starting to sink. He snatched at the items, but his struggling made his head go under again. No matter how hard he kicked, it seemed he was being dragged down. It felt as if someone were tugging on his feet!

And then he remembered the pouch full of coins. If he untied the pouch and let it go, he would probably bob to the surface. But the money! It wasn't his money—it was Ozawa-san's. And the money from Hideki's clothing, too! How would he ever earn enough to repay Ozawa and Hideki? It could take a lifetime!

On the other hand, if he drowned here and now, the money would go down with him anyway. Still, maybe it would be better to drown than to suffer the shame of losing Ozawa-san's goods and money.

But, oh! He wanted to take a breath! He wanted to live! He wanted to see what lay beyond the dark hills on the other side of the bay. If only, he thought, he could swim the way he had in his dream when he swam from star to star.

One thing was certain: Unless he let go of the money, both he and the money were doomed. He tore the pouch away from his sash, then kicked. As he rose up and up, he watched the coins drop from the pouch, glimmering like stars in a dark sky. They drifted down and down, glinted one last time, then disappeared into the murky depths.

15

LEAVING JAPAN

July 17, 1853

The squadron left the anchorage on Sunday morning, July 17. The four vessels began their voyage and started away rapidly without a yard of canvas set. The morning was fine, and as the departure of the Americans was a great event, and the appearance of the four ships moving off in stately procession, succeeding each other in regular line, was imposing and novel to the Japanese unfamiliar with the power of steam, crowds of people gathered upon the land to behold the sight. . . . The soldiers thronged out of the batteries and hurrying to the loftiest summits eagerly looked at the passing ships. As the squadron steamed out of the bay a parting look was obtained of the lofty summit of Mount Fuji, both behind and in advance.

—M. C. Perry, *Narrative of the Expedition to the China Seas and Japan, 1852–1854*

PART TWO
EARTH

Even a road of one thousand miles

can only be traversed by taking one step at a time.

—Miyamoto Musashi, *The Book of Five Rings*

16

THE TOKAIDO

The Month of Leaves, 6th Year of Kaei

There were opportunities along the Tokaido. Everyone always said so. After all, it was the main road leading to and away from Edo, and everyone who traveled had to use it, rich and poor, big and small, powerful or powerless.

The mighty lords were borne along in fine palanquins carried by four bearers and accompanied by hundreds of servants and retainers. Others traveled in simpler kagos, basket-like chairs suspended on poles carried by two men. There were samurai on horseback, and many others who walked and had very little in the way of baggage.

Yoshi was one of these. He had the clothes on his back and, fortunately, the somewhat rumpled travel permit. He had also managed to save one wrinkled, ragged print from his underwater adventure, which he had carefully unrolled and dried in the sun. That one print was the only thing he had left of Ozawa's art.

"No matter how hungry I get," Yoshi told himself, "I am not going to sell it."

There must be some kind of work he could do to earn back the money he'd lost, Yoshi thought as he trudged along the road. There were many, many travelers on the Tokaido, and travelers needed things. They needed a place to sleep, food to eat, entertainment, and new sandals when theirs wore out. He would find a way to earn money, and then he would return to Uraga and repay Ozawa-san.

His stomach rumbled as he passed by a man grilling eels. Then his mouth watered at the smell of toasted dengaku. He stopped to watch hungrily as men dipped the tofu cakes in a paste of fermented soybeans, but he turned away quickly before the warm food disappeared into their mouths.

Then, all of a sudden, there was the answer: a pleasant-looking man wearing a fuki-leaf hat, sitting among cypress

Travelers on the Tokaido. (*Katsushika Hokusai*)

trees, weaving straw into shoes. Well! If there was one thing Yoshi knew, it was shoes.

"Honorable sandal maker," Yoshi said, "please excuse my intrusion."

The sandal maker dropped his head in a cursory bow and kept at his work, expertly weaving the lengths of straw.

"You are very accomplished at your work, sir," Yoshi said.

The man crinkled his face and shook his head. "It is a lowly occupation," he replied.

Some scratchy thing dropped down the back of Yoshi's tunic, and he glanced up into the tree. He caught a glimpse of a little face. Just for an instant. Then the face disappeared among the branches.

Yoshi stepped out from under the tree and turned back to the sandal maker. "It is an honest occupation," he said, "for without sandals, what would happen to our poor feet?"

"Or our horses' feet," the man said.

"What?"

"These are shoes for horses." The man dangled a huge woven-straw shoe from his finger.

Of course! There were many horses along the Tokaido. Their hooves needed protection against the rocky ground. He'd seen strings of these shoes hanging at transport stations.

"Do you need an assistant?" Yoshi blurted out. "I know I

don't look like much, and, indeed, I am not much of anything. But I have experience with shoes."

"I'll tell you what," the sandal maker said. "I will give you four sandals to sell, and you will bring me the money you make. I am quite certain you will come back, because at the end of the day you are going to want nothing more than to return Chibi to me."

"Chibi?" Yoshi asked.

"Chibi-chan!" the sandal maker shouted up into the tree. In answer, there was a rain of pine needles and suddenly a small boy stood before Yoshi.

"Are you going to be my friend today?" the boy asked. Without an invitation, he climbed like a monkey onto Yoshi's back.

The sandal maker was right: Yoshi couldn't wait to return Chibi to him at the end of the day. Yoshi had sold only one sandal all day. The rest of the time he'd spent chasing the little boy, snatching him out of the road when horses came thundering by, coaxing him down from the roof of a food stall and out of trees, apologizing to people for his misbehavior, returning a peach that Chibi had stolen from a fruit vendor, and, sadly, using the money he'd earned from his one sandal sale to buy the crying Chibi a slice of bean jelly.

But Jiro the sandal maker was kind. He offered Yoshi a place to sleep in his little hut set back among the cypress trees.

"The Tokaido can be a dangerous place at night," he said.

Every day, Yoshi took Chibi and tried to sell horseshoes. But every day, he spent most of the time chasing after the little boy. By sundown, after Yoshi had paid the sandal maker, there were always just a few coins left. By the time he had bought something to eat, there was often not even enough money for a soak at the public bathhouse, where he might wash off the grit and dust from the day.

Then Yoshi discovered that he could do better business if he set himself up near the way station, where travelers exchanged their horses for fresh mounts or stopped to rest, water, or feed their horses. He offered to carry water or pick the stones out of the horses' hooves and was sometimes rewarded with a sale. When he found a long pole on which he could carry many sandals at a time, business began to really pick up.

He knew he should save all his money so he could someday have enough to repay Ozawa, but he had an idea of how he could earn even *more* money: He bought himself a yatate. The drawing kit had a perfect little inkwell and a small tube into which slid an equally small brush. He also purchased some mulberry-bark paper. While he waited for customers, he drew

A post station on the Tokaido. (*Ando Hiroshige*)

pictures. These he intended to sell and in this way earn even more money. He wasn't nearly as good as Ozawa, of course, but he had learned quite a bit from the artist. At least, he thought so.

At first, he tried drawing barbarians, but his potential customers scoffed at the pictures. "No," they said. "Barbarians have bigger noses than that. And they're hairier."

So he quit trying to draw barbarians and started drawing horses. This was easier because he could look at actual horses, and that helped. Sometimes he drew horses and sometimes he drew swords, and he imagined that soon people would pay a lot of money for his pictures and he would earn so much money that he could pay Ozawa back. *And* hire a babysitter for Chibi.

In the meantime, his pouch grew quite plump and full of

coins, and he liked to jingle it from time to time, imagining how it would be when he would one day have enough to repay both Ozawa and Hideki.

Things got even better when he found a big-branched tree and said to Chibi, "Climb up in that tree and call down to me if you see anyone on horseback." The little monkey scampered up the tree.

"What are you drawing?" Chibi called down to Yoshi from his perch in the tree one day.

"I am drawing a picture of a sword that will be so good that it will leap off the page and into my hand," Yoshi replied. "Then I'll draw myself a suit of armor and a helmet with huge stag horns coming out of the top, and all of it painted in red lacquer. Next I'll draw a horse that will whinny and prance out of the paper, and then I will ride away and fight the barbarians."

"Can I come, too?" Chibi asked from up in his tree.

"No," said a voice, none too kindly. Then *thud thud thud*. Footsteps approached.

Yoshi recognized the thudding footfall. He knew who it was without having to look up.

"So, Yoshitaro," Kitsune said, "you want to fight the barbarians."

Yoshi didn't answer. He didn't look up. He knew what the law said: "Common people who behave unbecomingly to a samurai or who do not show respect to their superiors may be cut down on the spot." Kitsune already had reason enough to cut him down.

So Yoshi held his tongue, and glanced wistfully at his drawings. If only, he thought, he was as good an artist as Sesshu Toyo had been, and his drawings could become real. What was it that Ozawa had said? Something about how much we fail to imagine is possible . . . ? He wished he could imagine something that would save him from Kitsune, because things did not look good for him right now.

"There was a time when you thought you were good enough to draw a sword," Kitsune said, pantomiming the drawing of a sword from its scabbard. "Now you can only *draw* a sword." He pretended to draw with a brush in the air, and laughed at his pun.

Again, Yoshi said nothing. There was a little shower of leaves from above, but Yoshi forced himself not to look up. He hoped Chibi would stay still and out of trouble up there.

"Hideki . . . ," Kitsune began, "because of you . . ."

Yoshi's heart nearly stopped beating. Because of him . . . what? Had Hideki been injured? Killed? What?

"Hideki wishes to become a monk!"

Yoshi almost clapped. That was a perfect thing for tender-hearted Hideki. He would be an excellent monk. And he would not have to fight.

Yoshi glanced up at Kitsune. A livid scar ran down one side of his face. *The scar I made*, Yoshi realized with horror.

"This is not what his father had in mind for his son," Kitsune said.

Yoshi lowered his eyes.

"What kind of a world do we live in when a son willfully goes against his father's wishes?"

Yoshi knew this was not a question that required an answer.

"You put him up to it!" Kitsune exclaimed. "It is your fault! His father brought him home from that temple, and now he has run away again. You have done this."

Yoshi shook his head. "I don't know anything—" he started.

"Hold your tongue, you impudent cur, or this is what will happen to you." Kitsune slid a straw sandal off the pole. He held it, dangling from one hand, and said in a low voice, "First I'll sever the tendon behind your knees, like this." He sliced through one of the straw straps. "Then I'll cut the tendon at your elbows." He snagged another sandal with his sword and sliced it apart. Then he took another one, tossed it up in the air, and slashed it to ribbons as it fell. He continued to destroy sandal after sandal this way.

Yoshi could not stand to watch. The ruin of the sandals was one thing, but for a samurai to use his sword for such a purpose—it was disgraceful. "No honorable samurai would use his sword that way," Yoshi scolded.

"What did you say, worm?" Kitsune spit out the words and stepped toward Yoshi.

At the same moment, a streak of color dropped from the tree and landed with a *plop!* on Kitsune's back. Kitsune twisted to grab at the little boy, whose arms were wrapped around the big man's neck.

Yoshi leaped up, snatched his sandal pole, and swung it into the back of Kitsune's knees. The big man went down, Chibi sprang away, and the two boys took off running. Kitsune staggered to his feet and followed.

The boys doubled back onto the road, with Kitsune close on their heels. That was why they didn't notice the kago until too late, when they were directly in its path. The kago bearers lurched to a halt, the samurai retainers following on foot also stopped, and the boys froze.

The man in the kago stuck his head out and asked, "What is going on here?" The boys dropped to their knees and pressed their foreheads to the ground.

"Tell the boys to come here," the man said.

Yoshi and Chibi crept to him on their knees, heads down.

"I will cut down these rude little peasants who have caused you distress," Kitsune told the man in the kago.

But the man held up his hand and said, "Please, put your sword away. I would like to talk with the boys."

Kitsune must have noticed the crest of the Lord of Tosa on the man's sleeve, because he slid his sword into its scabbard and stalked away, glancing back once to glower at Yoshi.

The man unfolded himself out of the kago and said to the boys, "Stand up now and tell me what happened. You darted into the road as if you were being chased by a tiger!"

"We were just minding our own business," Chibi blurted out, "selling horseshoes. See these fine horseshoes?" He held up a tattered sandal. "Very fine! Does your horse need shoes?"

"Honorable sir," Yoshi interrupted, "please excuse the ignorance of the little boy. Of course you have no need of horseshoes."

"Let me see." The man moved the boys and his small entourage to the side of the road—the opposite side from Kitsune, Yoshi noticed.

"I am sorry," Yoshi said. "The shoes have all been damaged." He slid the least-damaged one off the pole and handed it to the man, who examined it as if he'd never seen such a thing before. While the man was looking at it, Yoshi set the pole down.

"You know, in some places they make shoes for horses out of iron," the Tosa man said.

"Wouldn't that be terribly heavy?" Yoshi asked.

"Yes, but the shoe is not a shoe like this." The man held up one of the straw shoes. "It doesn't go all the way around the horse's hoof. It is worn only on the underside and is affixed with nails. It gives very strong protection to the horse's foot and lasts for a long time. They make them in the way a sword is made—heated in a forge, then hammered and bent into a shape like this." The man drew a half circle in the air.

"I have never heard of anything like that," Yoshi said. "What place is this where you saw such a thing?"

"Why, it was in America," the man said.

"America!" Yoshi whispered.

"Where the giants come from!" Chibi crowed, then started singing: "'They came from the land of darkness. Giants with hooked noses. Giants with rough hair, loose and red . . .'"

The man laughed. "Is that a popular song these days?"

Chibi continued singing: "'They danced with joy as they sailed away to the distant land of darkness.'"

"Do you want to hear a song from that 'land of darkness'?" the man asked.

Chibi hushed instantly and stared at the Tosa man, who cleared his throat. "*Ohhh . . . ,*" he began, singing in English, "*I come from Alabama, with a banjo on my knee. I'm going to Louisiana, my true love for to see . . .*"

Yoshi and Chibi stood in shocked silence, their mouths impolitely agape. Then Yoshi said, "I saw the outsiders myself. And their ships, too."

"Did you?" The man bent down toward him. "Tell me about it."

Out of the corner of his eye, Yoshi watched Kitsune. He had retreated to the shadows and sat, madly shredding grass in his hand, tearing it into tiny pieces. *What he wishes he were doing to me!* Yoshi thought.

So Yoshi took his time, telling the man from Tosa every detail he could remember and hoping that Kitsune would grow tired of waiting and just go away.

"I will show you a picture," Yoshi said. He pulled out the one wrinkled, rumpled picture he'd salvaged from his underwater adventure. It was printed with the image of a person who seemed half animal, half man. Fur-like hair sprouted from everywhere: his head and all over his face, too. His eyes were huge and fierce, his nose immense, his face as creased as the paper.

An anonymous Japanese artist's interpretation of a "foreign barbarian."
The commentary claims it's a "true portrait of Perry."

The Tosa man hooted. "This is a silly rendering. This looks like a tengu—a demon. Americans don't look like that."

"Yes, they do!" Yoshi blurted out. "I know, for I saw them myself. And they look just like that."

"Boy!" said one of the man's retainers. "Remember your place."

Yoshi quickly lowered his gaze and held his tongue.

"Let him speak," the Tosa man said.

"What does he know?" the retainer complained. "He's only a boy making up stories."

"Let him say what he knows," the man insisted.

"They have bits of round jewelry on their jackets," Yoshi said.

"Those are called *buttons*," the man said.

"*Buttons* . . . ," Yoshi repeated. "And they put their hands into their clothes and they disappear into pouches sewn right into their clothing."

"*Pockets*," the man said.

"*Pockets*," Yoshi repeated.

The man smiled and said, "I remember myself at your age, learning these same words."

"You were just my age when you went to America?" Yoshi asked.

"How old are you?" the man asked him.

"Thirteen," Yoshi said. He frowned. "Or thereabouts."

"Yes, I was about that age. Perhaps a little older. And I was just a poor fisherman's son from Tosa. But in America, I had a horse with iron shoes."

"You had your own horse?"

"Yes," the man said. "Anyone can have a horse in America, gentlemen and farmers, rich and not so rich. Would you like a horse of your own?"

"He has a horse," Chibi chirped, holding up Yoshi's drawing.

"Did you draw this?" the Tosa man asked Yoshi. "Very well done. You are a bright boy, I can see. And you are going to grow up to see great change. There is a big world out there—a big, new world, and you will have the opportunity to see it."

Yoshi listened to the man in silence. Was he kind of crazy? People were not allowed to leave Japan, even if they *wanted* to go. Didn't he know the edict that said that anyone who tried to leave the country would be put to death? And no one had ever called him "bright" before. The man talked strangely, too. In addition to his Tosa accent, he had a funny way of talking. And it was impossible to tell if he was a samurai or not. He wore the samurai's haori and hakama, and his two retainers were samurai, but the Tosa man carried no swords. Not only that, he lowered himself to converse with a poor peasant boy like Yoshi. He *must* be at least a little bit crazy.

Still, it was as if he had looked into Yoshi's heart and read his secret desire to see more of the world.

"How . . . ," Yoshi started. He hesitated, not sure if he was even legally permitted to ask such a question. "How did you get to America?" he blurted.

"That is a long story, which I hope to share with you another time. But right now, I feel quite tired, and would like to rest. In fact," he said to his retainers, "there's a fine-looking inn, right there." He turned back to Yoshi and Chibi, bid them good-bye, and walked toward the inn, humming. Humming, right out in public!

"He's gone," Chibi said.

"Gone?" Yoshi asked absently.

"The bad man. He went away while you were talking."

Yoshi had almost forgotten about Kitsune. "Good," he said. "Let's get back to work."

As they went to fetch the sandal pole, Yoshi thought about some of the strange things the Tosa man seemed to know: words and songs and humming.

Yoshi tried humming a little, and was still humming when he reached for his sandal pole. But when he saw the pole, dangling with ruined sandals, his smile faded and the song died on his lips. How could he have forgotten what a sorry mess he'd made of things? He was already in debt to Ozawa. Now he was further indebted to Jiro. He slid the ruined sandals off the pole and threw them into the bushes.

"Come on," he said to Chibi. "I'll take you home."

Back at the cypress grove, Jiro sat, still working away. Yoshi set the empty pole on the ground and kneeled before him.

"You must have met with good fortune," Jiro said, smiling at the sight of the empty pole.

"No, Jiro-san," Yoshi said. "I am a miserable failure. All the good sandals you made were ruined by a bully on the road because of my stupidity. But I will pay for them!" He still had the coins that he had been saving, and he counted out the exact number to cover the cost of all the shoes he had lost. He handed the money to Jiro. Then, because there really wasn't quite enough, he also gave Jiro his drawing kit.

Jiro looked at the coins, then handed two of them back to Yoshi.

"Here," he said. "Take Chibi to the public bath. You both could use one."

17

AT THE PUBLIC BATH

Steam rose from the large pool of hot water and from the bare heads and bodies of the bathers. The steam was so heavy, it obscured all but the closest bathers, but their voices were clear. Yoshi could only make out the tops of their heads, some of which were bald except for the topknots. Even naked, you could always tell a samurai by his topknot. A group of samurai, merchants, and artisans were all conversing about . . . what else? The coming barbarian invasion. Was Kitsune among them? Yoshi couldn't tell.

"Perhaps the divine wind will come again to save us from the barbarians," one of the bathers said. "It saved us before!" It was not Kitsune's voice.

"That was five hundred years ago!" a wheezy voice scoffed. Also not Kitsune. "But one thing is sure, we must drive them away now, or we will never have another chance."

That's right, Yoshi thought.

"And the only way to rid the country of them is by force," a man with a deep, rumbly voice said. Not Kitsune.

Yoshi agreed with that, too. Japan's warriors must drive the outsiders away.

Having determined that Kitsune was not among the men present, he plunked Chibi on a stool and sat on one himself, and they began to scrub themselves clean before entering the pool.

"Our warriors are not well trained anymore," said yet another voice. "Many have become lazy. There are quite a few who have sold their armor and even their swords to pay their debts."

As Yoshi scrubbed Chibi's back with a bag of rice bran, he thought, *If I were allowed to carry a sword, it would not matter how hungry I got. I would never, ever sell it. How could a true samurai ever sell his katana?*

"It seems impossible," the gruff voice was saying. "We have no real army, and our coastal defenses are in shambles."

"What if we just let them in?" said a soft but clear voice. "Without fighting? Maybe nothing would happen."

"How can you say such a thing?" crowed the wheezy voice. His face appeared out of the steam, rosy and pink. "They will destroy our way of life. Would we have to succumb to their barbaric ways?"

Yoshi tried to picture the foreigners walking around in their country. He shuddered at the thought of having to look upon those creatures on a daily basis, with their sharp, beak-like noses, wicked-looking eyes, and bristly faces!

He couldn't get the picture out of his head, and he barely heard the men as they discussed the possibility of the Americans being contained on their own separate little island, as the Dutch traders were on the island of Dejima.

"Perhaps the Americans can supply us with the few goods we desire, as the Dutch have done for us," one of the men suggested.

But it was generally agreed that the American barbarians had already proved their unwillingness to conform to the laws of the land, and probably wouldn't comply the way the Dutch had done.

"There has to be a way of using their thinking without becoming like them," a man said, draping a towel over his head. "There must be some kind of compromise."

"Compromise? Never! Are we not samurai?"

"*That* we may be, but are we also idiots?" the other man countered, complacently rubbing a wet towel over his face. "We either compromise or are crushed. What I'm saying is that we need to learn their ways in order to know how to get rid of them! We need expert help. We need people who have firsthand knowledge of Western might and military power, who understand ships and guns."

"You're talking about that fellow who went to America and came back," said the rumbly one.

Yoshi scrubbed more slowly so he could listen.

"It is said he is traveling the Tokaido now, under protection of the shogun," said the wheezy one, who then coughed.

Yoshi stopped scrubbing and listened harder. Were they talking about the man he and Chibi had met on the road?

"But he is just a commoner," said Rumbly Voice. "His name is Manjiro. His *only* name."

Yoshi led Chibi to the pool and slipped into the water, edging closer to the conversation. The men took no notice of the two small boys.

"He has been granted samurai status," the soft-voiced man was saying. "The lowest rank, I think. But he is allowed to carry the daisho, and I have heard he will be allowed to take a second name."

"That is because the shogun wants him as an adviser," said a young man with glistening hair, sitting on the edge of the pool.

So the Tosa man was going to Edo, Yoshi thought.

"Adviser to the shogun! What kind of world is this, in which I, a loyal retainer to Lord Shimazu, must bow to an outsider?" a red-faced bushi said.

"Shh," said a voice out of the steam. "The shogun's spies are everywhere."

"Well," said yet another voice, "he isn't really an outsider. He was born in Tosa somewhere."

"He's as good as an outsider," said Rumbly Voice. "He was shipwrecked and plucked off an island by the barbarians. He owes his life to them—thus he owes his loyalty to them."

"He has only been back in our country for a couple of years," commented Red Face. "Perhaps it is *he* who has brought the foreign ships to our shores."

"He can only have been sent here as a spy," agreed Wheezy One.

Really? Yoshi wondered. The man he'd met had not seemed like a spy.

But those around him murmured their assent, and that he was a danger to everyone.

"He is on his way to Edo." The deep, rumbling voice had lowered itself to an ominous whisper. "He could be here, among us!"

"He *is* here!" Chibi piped up.

"What? What's that you say, boy?" Wheezy One asked, turning his attention to Chibi.

"He's right here. Not in this bath, but we saw him today— didn't we, Yoshi-san?"

Yoshi tried to swallow, but he felt as if he had something lodged in his throat.

"Yoshi? Didn't we?" Chibi prodded.

"No, I don't think so," Yoshi said. "I think they're talking about someone else."

"No, Yoshi," Chibi insisted. "That is the man they're talking about."

"Is that true, boy?" Rumbly Voice asked.

Once again, Yoshi hesitated.

Chibi did not. "Yes! Yes!" he chirped. "We talked to him! He comes from Tosa! He rides in a kago! He said Yoshi was a bright boy."

Yoshi didn't think he could deny it now, after Chibi had made such a thorough description. He nodded.

"And you know where he is staying?"

Yoshi hesitated.

During the pause, Red Face whispered harshly, "Our country should be protected against such a man."

"He's staying at the Edge of the River Inn," Chibi crowed.

"You, boy," Rumbly Voice said, addressing Yoshi. "Go and tell him there are some . . . admirers who would like to . . . speak with him. Ask him to meet us at the hour of the boar at the Seven Grasses Teahouse. Then come back and tell us what he says. When you return, I'll give you a string of copper pennies for your trouble."

Chibi had already scrambled out of the pool, and Yoshi now followed. He hastily wrapped Chibi in his tunic, slipped into his own clothes, then hustled the small boy toward the cypress grove. Here and there, paper lanterns bobbed as people came and went. Yoshi tried to peer at their faces, making sure Kitsune was not among them.

He dropped the protesting Chibi at Jiro's hut and continued on the dark path to the inn where Manjiro was staying. It would be nice to get those copper pennies, he thought, now that he had no money at all. Even if they were only pennies, it would be something.

But it didn't feel right. Leaves turning in the breeze seemed to *tsk-tsk* their disapproval. Even the crickets along the path seemed to scold him. "*Should not, would not, should not, would not,*" they sang. What should he do? he wondered. He was sure the men in the bath meant to harm the Tosa man. To whom did he owe his loyalty? Did he not owe his own countrymen his allegiance? But the Tosa man had done him no harm. And, after all, he, too, was a countryman.

And then he found himself standing outside the man's room. "Excuse my intrusion, um . . ." Yoshi wasn't sure how to address an outsider. ". . . sir," he whispered at the door. He would just warn him, that's all. Just tell him that there were those who wished him harm. This is what he intended. But the door slid open, and the man stood there, a black silhouette framed from behind by lantern light. The light spilled out the door, rolling out of the room and up to Yoshi's feet like a glowing path.

Even though Yoshi knew it was just a room in an inn, a room like any other, something made it seem as if past that open door he could see all the way to Edo, and even beyond that, maybe to worlds beyond Japan.

18

A FROG JUMPS IN

An angry rumbling came from the front of the inn. The rattling of the gate rattled Yoshi's very bones.

"It's them!" Yoshi told the man named Manjiro. "It's the men from the bath, the ones who said they want to speak with you." He bit his lip. "You stay here," he said. "I'll go."

He marched out as bravely as he could but quailed when he saw the men assembled at the front gate of the inn: Rumbly Voice, with hands on hips; Wheezy One, with arms crossed over an ample stomach; another, with thumbs hitched in his sash; and yet another, with hands tucked into his sleeves. The red-faced one, whom Yoshi kept his eye on, rested his hand on the hilt of his sword.

"Well, little ragamuffin," Hand-on-Hilt said. "We went to the teahouse, but you did not appear."

"I had to take the little boy home to his father," Yoshi said. "Then I came straight here. But the Tosa man is not—" He was about to say "here," when Manjiro walked out of the inn, smiled at the group, and bowed politely.

Yoshi stiffened. He glanced around for something with

which to defend the two of them, and seeing nothing, eyed the swords of the bushi gathered there. Five bushi; five katanas. Even in his wildest fantasies, Yoshi had never taken on that many opponents. And he didn't have a sword, of course. Not even a bamboo one. Neither did the Tosa man.

"Honorable gentlemen," Manjiro said. "What an honor that you grace me with your presence!"

Yoshi glanced nervously at him, then at the group of men. Fresh from the hot spring, their cheeks rosy, their hair damp, they had the appearance of well-scrubbed schoolboys.

"How kind of you to arrive just now when I was puzzling over the meaning of a haiku by Basho," Manjiro said. "Perhaps you know it? It goes like this: 'The ancient pond / A frog jumps in / The sound of the water.'" He smiled.

There was a moment of silence. Shuffling of feet. Then Rumbly Voice cleared his throat and growled, "The ancient pond represents the eternal."

"Yes, that is how I understand it," agreed Wheezy One. "The timeless, motionless component of water."

"And the frog?" Manjiro asked.

"I believe the frog represents the temporary, the momentary element," said Hand-on-Hilt.

"And the sound of the water," said Wheezy One, "is that

moment when the temporary element intersects with the eternal."

"Splash!" exclaimed Rumbly Voice, clapping his hands for emphasis.

"What happens as soon as the frog is underwater?" Manjiro asked.

"The pond becomes still once again?" Yoshi offered.

"Is the pond the same as it was?"

There was silence as they all pondered this question.

"No!" Yoshi exclaimed. "Because now there is a frog in it!"

"Ah," said Manjiro. "But is that a bad thing? Or a good thing?"

There was some argument among the men as to whether the introduction of the frog to the pond was a good or a bad thing. Yoshi thought it was a good thing, for, after all, what is a pond without a frog?

Manjiro thanked the men for helping him puzzle out the deeper significance of the haiku and invited them into the front garden, saying, "No doubt you came to hear of that faraway land of America." Without waiting for a reply, he began to tell them fantastic things. How there was something called a railroad that moved so fast that the countryside became just a blur, and about how gold had been discovered in a place called California and ordinary people had become as rich as the great lords who traveled the Tokaido. "Some are so rich they ride in carriages with silver wheels!" he said.

After the men finally drifted away to their inns or homes, Manjiro said to Yoshi, "You are a brave fellow, to face those men alone. Fortunately, their bark was worse than their bite."

Their bark worse than their bite? That must be a barbarian saying, Yoshi thought.

"But now you must run home to your parents before they become worried about you," Manjiro finished.

"I regret to admit I have neither home nor parents," Yoshi said.

"I am sorry to hear that," Manjiro said. He turned his gaze on the garden, its bare stalks lit by the blue moonlight. His thoughts seemed to be far away. Then he turned back to Yoshi, smiled, and said, "I hope that someday your heart will find a home."

Home, Yoshi thought. The word tasted as sweet as a plum when you said it, but what did it really mean?

19

YOSHI THE BODYGUARD

It was the season of the Seven Grasses of Autumn. In the low-lying lands, fields of rice were ready for harvest. In the higher lands, winter wheat had been sown. And higher yet on the hills, the trees were frosted with white.

Yoshi took in a great lungful of air and let it out in a poof of white smoke. Steam, he thought. Somehow it could power ships. This was something he would like to understand.

His heart swelled a little to think that he was no longer Yoshi the Nobody. He was now a bodyguard for a bushi. After the men from the bath had left, and after Manjiro had asked Yoshi about his home and family, Manjiro had said, "Perhaps, if you are alone, you would like to take a job as my bodyguard."

Yoshi laughed out loud. "Now you are making fun of me."

"Not at all," Manjiro said. "I believe you have already earned yourself that position. You have just done me a great service by warning me of danger. By contrast, think of those two who travel with me. They have slept through the whole thing!" He laughed.

Yoshi couldn't help smiling. "But I am just a boy and a peasant!" he said. "One must be a samurai to be a bodyguard. Even if I were big enough to defend you, what would I use as a weapon? I have no swords."

"Let us just say you are an *apprentice* bodyguard, then," Manjiro said.

"Your retainers won't like it," Yoshi said, keeping his voice low.

"Oh, we shan't tell them," Manjiro said. "There's no need for them to know what your job is. Once we get to Edo, we'll get you an even better position. Let's see. You seem to like horses. Maybe a job at the shogun's stables?"

The shogun's stables! Yoshi thought. Something he never would have imagined.

Yet now, after saying good-bye to Jiro and Chibi, he was on his way to Edo—as a bodyguard! Never mind that it was a secret. Never mind that he was only a scrawny thirteen-year-old peasant. A scrawny peasant without a weapon. Never mind that nobody else knew—or ever would know—of his position. It still made him feel as if he carried a little treasure—a little secret treasure. He walked a little taller, felt a little stronger. Maybe there was even a bit of a swagger in his step.

◆ ◆ ◆

"Have you been to Edo?" Manjiro asked Yoshi.

"Oh, sure," Yoshi said, trying to sound casual, as if he'd been there many times.

"Excellent!" Manjiro said. "I have never been, and you can show me the sights and help me find my way around."

Yoshi nodded, although not very confidently. Of course he didn't know his way around Edo! All he knew was what he had learned from Ozawa's map. Why had he said such a stupid thing? He had not expected that Manjiro, who was about to become an adviser to the shogun, would want to be shown around Edo by a mere boy like him!

But in the days on the Tokaido that followed, Manjiro often walked alongside Yoshi, saying he preferred walking to jouncing along in a kago. "It's not quite like a ride in a carriage, is it?" he said. To this, Yoshi had no answer, because he had no idea what a carriage was.

Manjiro seemed to enjoy telling Yoshi stories of that distant land, America. When they passed by merchants selling rice cakes and simmered burdock root, Manjiro said that in America they ate something called "bread" and drank a thing called "coffee."

"But boys your age are expected to drink *milk*," Manjiro said.

"Miruku," Yoshi repeated. "What is it?"

"You wouldn't like it," Manjiro said.

Yoshi did not doubt that.

After Yoshi and Manjiro had bowed to several high-ranking officials who passed by, Manjiro said, "Americans do not bow to each other as we do. Instead, they shake hands. When a guest enters the home of an American, he takes off his hat. They sit on chairs instead of on the floor."

It was odd, Yoshi thought, that his new master wanted to spend time with a peasant boy instead of his samurai retainers, closer to him in age and status. But there were many odd things about the man . . . something a little off, something not entirely Japanese. It was hard to put his finger on it exactly. Maybe he was a bit too bold, too forward. He didn't come toward people with a readiness to bow—he looked them in the face and seemed always ready to thrust out his hand in that strange way the barbarians greeted each other—clasping each other's hand and pumping their arms up and down. It was a graceless gesture, entirely barbaric.

Oddest of all, Manjiro didn't wear his swords. This made Yoshi nervous. He worried for the man's safety, especially because of things he had noticed.

First it was just a glimpse of a fluttering sleeve, and the shape of a person slipping in among a group of white-clad pilgrims. Yoshi noticed the suddenly cast-down eyes of a man supposedly reading a broadsheet, and a door sliding open a crack as they approached, then sliding shut as they passed by.

Yoshi was sure they were being watched. Perhaps they were being followed. He remembered the words of the men in the bath: "The shogun's spies are everywhere." Is that who was following them? Or was it someone who wished them harm? And if it was, how was Yoshi going to defend his master?

"Honorable employer," Yoshi said when he couldn't hold his tongue any longer, "as your, um, bodyguard, or . . . er . . . *apprentice* bodyguard, I have to humbly request that you wear at least one of your swords."

"Oh? Why?"

"There are several reasons, the main one being that you might protect yourself with it."

"That's hardly likely," Manjiro said. "I have no idea how to use it!"

"Well, you don't want to be mistaken for a commoner, do you?"

Manjiro shrugged. It was an American gesture that Yoshi had come to understand meant "I don't know" or "I don't care either way." Yoshi wasn't sure which shrug this one was.

"You could be cut down by mistake!" Yoshi cried. "If a bushi were not to know who you were. Or he could use the excuse of not realizing who you were to cut you down."

"The sword is not the solution to everything," Manjiro said. "Have you not heard of the spirit of winning without the sword?"

"Yes," Yoshi said, "but . . ."

"I want to be known as a man of peace," Manjiro went on. "How do I express that if I am wearing a sword?"

"I didn't want to say," Yoshi said, "but we are being watched. Perhaps followed."

"People are curious," Manjiro said. "They just want to take a look. And, as we know," he added cheerily, "the shogun's spies are everywhere."

Well, as odd as the man might seem, it was not Yoshi's place to argue with him. If it were Yoshi who had the right to wear a sword, well . . . ! He would wear it proudly. He would use his swords to fight with honor!

Part of the procession of a great lord. (*Utagawa Hiroshige III*)

"And, anyway," Manjiro said, "why do I need a sword if I am protected by such a resourceful bodyguard as you?"

"B-b-but," Yoshi stammered, "I can't carry swords, either! How am I to protect you?"

"I have faith in you, my friend," Manjiro said. "If it becomes necessary, you will find a way."

"Be down!" came the shout of a great lord's forerunners, and Yoshi watched the wave of commoners—food and charcoal vendors, jugglers, beggars, storytellers, and peddlers—drop to their knees as troops and officers appeared.

"This reminds me of a cattle drive," Manjiro said. "I saw one when I was in California. I learned to use a lasso from an old cowboy there. Here, I'll show you." He retrieved a length of rope from his belongings. He made a loop in it with a kind of knot that could slide up or down the length of the rope, which made the loop larger or smaller. "You never know when a lasso might come in handy," he said.

Yoshi kept one nervous eye on Manjiro, who was making slow circles over his head with the rope, and the other eye on the procession, where horses were parading by loaded with the great lord's baggage. Yoshi should be on his knees by now.

"How about if I try to rope one of those horses?" Manjiro asked.

Yoshi looked at him with horror, and Manjiro did an odd thing with one of his eyes. He closed it, then opened it—very quickly—while looking straight at Yoshi. Then he said, "What do you make of all this?"

"What do I make of what?" Yoshi asked.

"The parade." Manjiro nodded at the porters weighed down with lacquered chests, trunks, and baskets.

"Be down!" the bannermen roared.

Finally Manjiro bowed and Yoshi dropped to his knees, with his head inches from the ground. He could no longer see anything but the dirt, but he could hear the thud of feet, the clopping of hooves, the grunts and heavy breathing of the porters and then the palanquin bearers who would be carrying the great lord himself.

After the lord would come his hat bearer and his umbrella bearer. More trunks. Pages. More horses, more baggage, still more horses with their grooms and footmen, the lord's household servants, and other lower officers of his court. All the while, Yoshi stared at the dirt.

After the last of the entourage had passed by and Yoshi had risen and dusted himself off, Manjiro said, "Quite a show, isn't it?"

Yoshi glanced at him. The man's mouth was pressed into a

puckered disguise of a smile. He seemed to find all this rather amusing.

"And for what?" Manjiro asked. "That is something you start to wonder after a while: What is its purpose?"

"Purpose?" Yoshi didn't understand.

"This lasso has a useful purpose," Manjiro said, holding up the rope. Then he gestured to the procession that was disappearing around a bend and said, "But what was the purpose of all that?"

Yoshi had no answer, nor did he even really understand the question.

20

IN THE SHOGUN'S CASTLE

The Month of Frost, 6th Year of Kaei
(November 1853)

Yoshi never, ever would have imagined that he—*he!* Yoshi the Nobody!—would be seeing the inside of the shogun's castle! Except that he wasn't *seeing* anything, because he didn't dare lift his head for an instant.

Moving through the castle's quiet corridors, all Yoshi saw were his feet. And Manjiro's feet. And the smooth stones, polished wooden boards, or thick tatami mats of the floor beneath his feet. And occasionally someone else's feet whispering past.

He did not see the scenes by famous artists hanging in the alcoves of the rooms. He didn't see the elegant flower arrangements, or the vast gardens, or the rich brocade or embroidered silk kimonos of those who passed by.

Nor did he hear much. It seemed that in the shogun's castle all that could be heard were whispers: the soft whisper of paper doors sliding open or shut. The whispers of silken garments and stockinged feet in the passageways. The whispers of voices. Urgent whispers.

Not until Yoshi was seated outside the reception room, where Manjiro was meeting with Magistrate Kawaji and other high-level officials of the Bakufu, was he really able to listen. And thanks to the paper walls, he could hear some of what was being discussed.

Manjiro began telling councillors that America was a very powerful nation made up of thirty-one states. He went on to describe its national resources: gold, silver, copper, iron, timber, and so on. As for agriculture, he said that the country grew abundant wheat, barley, corn, beans, and vegetables—but not rice, because they did not eat it there.

"It has been a long-cherished desire on the part of America to establish friendly relations with Japan," Manjiro said. "If a whaleship is delayed by a storm, Americans seek permission to get water and food here. In spite of their humble requests, if an American vessel is shipwrecked in Japanese waters, the survivors are treated harshly, as if they were beasts, by the Japanese authorities."

"Not so!" one of the councillors protested.

Yoshi heard the rustle of paper—a scroll being unrolled, he imagined.

"We received this at the arrival of the Black Ships," a

councillor was saying. "These drawings show the guns and weapons of the Americans."

Yoshi remembered Ozawa saying that the Bakufu was interested in pictures of the barbarian ships. He wondered if they were looking at Ozawa's drawings!

"More and more fighting ships and merchant ships driven by steam engines are being built in America," Manjiro explained. "These ships can be navigated in all directions, regardless of the wind or the current." He went on to tell about the firepower found on an American man-of-war: cannon and carronades, howitzers, muskets, pistols, and sabers. He finished by saying, "There are hardly any weapons that would frighten the Americans out of their wits."

The tone of the councillors' responses grew gloomy. "It is a thousand pities that we were not ready with our own military," one of them intoned.

Yoshi looked through the open doors at the somber colors and bare stalks of the late autumn garden, and the heavy gray sky above. Even in the midst of all this beauty and splendor, he thought, the prevalent tone was gloom.

"One thing Americans are not well trained in is swordsmanship," Manjiro said. "In my opinion, in close fighting, a samurai could easily take on three Americans."

There was a murmur of approval from the councillors.

"But America is working to develop its own country and has no time to attack other nations," Manjiro went on.

At this, there seemed to be an audible sigh of relief from the gathered officials.

"They are constantly learning, and their knowledge gets better and better," Manjiro continued. "Their fighting, merchant, and steam ships go all over the world. The Americans have learned the method of navigation by observing the heavenly bodies—as have I. If I had a ship," he said, "I could sail it to any part of the world."

Yoshi tried to imagine being able to do that—it was frightening to think about, because he had heard that monsters lived in the far reaches of the sea. And barbarians, of course. He shivered a little and turned back to listening while pretending not to.

He pretended a little harder, for he suddenly had the distinct impression that he was being watched. He turned his head just in time to catch a glimpse of a slippered foot disappearing around a corner.

21

THE STABLEBOY

It was late fall, and the air was pungent with the sour tang of fallen leaves and, for Yoshi, horses. Horses, and leather bridles and harnesses, straw and hay, and right now the heady and slightly sweet aroma of stewing grain.

He poured steaming water into a tub of feed, making a thick, warm porridge for the horses that had been training earlier in the day. The smell of it made his mouth water; it was all he could do not to scoop up a mouthful for himself. The slurry smelled—and looked—better than his own breakfast had that morning. It felt as if days had passed since he'd eaten the watery soup and cold rice in the barracks where he slept and ate with the other stable hands and workers.

Horses up and down the long building stuck their heads over their stall doors, all wondering, Yoshi supposed, if this deliciousness was meant for them. Nearby, a dappled mare stared at him intently. He stirred the porridge slowly, listening to the conversation of the other stableboys, who, finished with their chores, leaned against stall doors and chatted.

"I have thought of a way to conquer the red-hairs," one of the boys said. "When they come back."

"How?" said a round-faced boy. "Tell us!"

Yoshi stopped stirring.

"I have heard that the barbarians cannot bend their legs," the first boy said.

Yoshi glanced at the mare. Her dark eyes seemed to reflect his own amusement.

"That is true, Hiko," said the round-faced boy. "Those who have seen the Dutchmen riding in kagos say that their legs stick straight out, so it must be true."

"So," said the boy called Hiko, "the way to conquer them is simple. Cut bamboo lengths and spread them on the ground."

"Huh?" a little boy wondered.

"Oh!" exclaimed a boy whose hair stuck out in all directions. "I get it! When the hairy ones invade our land, they will slip on the bamboo and fall down, and, because they can't bend their legs, they won't be able to get up!"

"And then our warriors will chop them to pieces!" Hiko finished.

The other boys agreed that it was an excellent idea.

"That won't work," Yoshi said, "because the red-hairs can bend their legs as well as anyone."

Fanciful images of "foreign barbarians." (*Katsushika Hokusai*)

"Well, *honorable* Yoshi," Hiko said sarcastically, "who says the red-haired devils can bend their legs?"

"I do," Yoshi said. "I've seen them myself."

"Is that so?" Hiko said. "And where was that?"

"Uraga." Yoshi watched their expressions: for a moment impressed, because he had seen the barbarians. But then sneers appeared on the boys' faces.

"Is that where you're from?" Hiko asked, smiling smugly. "We figured you weren't from Edo."

Yoshi wondered what had given him away. Some slightly different way of dressing or wearing his hair? Did he have a noticeable accent?

"You came with the outsider, didn't you?" Hiko said.

"He's not an outsider. He is our countryman," Yoshi answered.

"He might as well be an outsider," said a small boy, emboldened by the older boy's words. "In the years he was away, he forgot everything. I heard that when he was presented with the two swords, he carried them home wrapped in a towel!"

"He was only a fisherman before, this *Manjiro*," said Hiko. "He is really just a peasant!"

"He isn't a peasant anymore," Yoshi protested. "He is a

bushi, and now the shogun has allowed him to take a second name. And that is the proper way for you to address him: *Nakahama* Manjiro."

Hiko's eyes flashed at Yoshi. He said, "My father says that in the case of that man, some mistake has been made. But the shogun will soon come to his senses and dismiss him."

"Maybe he has important information to impart," Yoshi said.

The boys howled with laughter.

"Like what? How to grow a big nose?" one boy cried.

"How to make yourself stink?" said the little boy, Han.

They squeezed their noses with their fingers.

This was not going to be as friendly an interchange as he had hoped, Yoshi realized. Should he leave now or stick it out a little longer? It would be nice to have some friends. Maybe if he joined in with them . . . It wasn't as if he, too, didn't think the man was strange. He even agreed with some of the things the boys said. So he laughed a little and said, "I admit he's a bit odd."

"What other strange things does he do?" the boys wanted to know. They leaned in, smiling.

"He does this funny thing with his eyes where he closes one of them, then opens it, while looking at you. Just one eye. Closed, then opened." Yoshi tried to imitate it, and the boys laughed.

"Maybe it's like a secret signal or something," Han said.

The other boys mumbled their agreement and turned back to Yoshi.

Their attitude toward him seemed to have changed, and Yoshi didn't feel like such an outcast now. So he went on: "The Tosa man could have ridden in a kago all the way to Edo, but he walked instead. He spent all his time talking to me instead of his samurai retainers. Like he couldn't tell that they were more important than I am."

Yoshi felt a little sorry to have said this. It was true; it was a strange way for a samurai to behave. Still, Manjiro *had* made Yoshi feel special. And how was Yoshi repaying him? By making fun of him.

He mumbled something about needing to finish, opened the stall door, picked up the tub of feed, and went in. The mare, Haru, turned and nudged him with her nose. But he found he couldn't look at her, or at her big, sad eyes.

22

KIKU

It snows,
And flowers
Unknown to spring
Blossom on the trees and grass,
Still sleeping through the winter
—Ki no Tsurayuki

Snow lay heaped on every twig and branch, thickening shrubs and trees as if it were full summer and the leaves and flowers had all blossomed white.

Behind the snow-laden shrubs, there was a spot in the garden private enough for Yoshi to practice his sword fighting in secret. He had a length of bamboo he kept hidden in Haru's stall, and when the opportunity arose, he practiced.

As graceful as a bird landing on water, Yoshi reminded himself as he pulled his "katana" from his sash. *That is how your movements with your sword should be. Your mind should be like water,* he told himself—realizing that if he had to tell himself that, then his mind was *not* like water.

He started again, drawing his bamboo sword and bowing to it. But just as he was about to begin, he heard voices coming from the other side of the hedge. He didn't think much of it until one of the voices said, "He knows much. He speaks and understands English and the ways of the Westerners." It was Lord Egawa who was speaking. He had taken a strong interest in Manjiro and his knowledge of the West. He had even invited Manjiro to stay in his compound.

Yoshi slowly lowered his bamboo katana. There were people—a group of officials, it sounded like—right on the other side of the hedge. He moved a little closer.

"He should be our official interpreter," Egawa said.

"I agree," said another voice. "He will help us not lose face by seeming ignorant."

Yoshi edged even closer.

An officious voice said, "He is too sympathetic to the American devils. He owes a debt of gratitude to them. If he were to be in the presence of the barbarians, they might kidnap him and take him aboard one of their ships."

"I do not think that Manjiro has any thoughts of treason," another voice was saying, "but upon getting on board, there is no telling what might happen. We do not know what method he might use in talking to the men on the ships."

Through the snowy branches, Yoshi noticed movement,

and he peeked through them to see a girl about his age sweeping the snow from the stepping-stones. She would only really sweep during the pauses, he noticed. Otherwise, she was only pretending to sweep.

She's a spy! he thought, then quickly changed his mind. No, that couldn't be right. She was only a girl! But the more he watched, the more convinced he became. Especially since she seemed to be silently moving closer to the hedge.

He was about to tiptoe away when a loud voice proclaimed, "Of course, nobody wants to be under the thumb of the West! But what can we do? We haven't the firepower, the military, to deal with them!"

Now the girl was so close, Yoshi couldn't escape his hiding spot without being seen. So he decided to act like he belonged there. He shoved his bamboo stick under the shrubs, crossed his arms, and took an attitude of, well . . . belonging. At least he hoped that's what he looked like.

Meanwhile, the men on the other side of the hedge continued their discussion.

"Time is essential if we are to complete our coastal defenses. Let us forestall the foreigners. Then, at some future time, we will find opportunity to reimpose the ban and forbid foreigners to come to Japan."

The girl was so close now, Yoshi could speak quietly to

her without being overheard. "You're listening in on their conversation!" he whispered.

"As are you," she whispered back.

"That's different," he said.

"Why?" she asked. "Because I am only a girl?"

"Well, that's true, isn't it?" he said.

She raised a very expressive eyebrow.

"Who are you spying for?" she asked.

He couldn't tell her that he was Manjiro's bodyguard and, as such, he needed to know if others were plotting against him. She would never believe that. Anyway, why should he tell her anything?

They glared at each other. She was only the gardener's daughter, he thought. She needn't act so high and mighty. Then she grinned, not bothering to politely hide her mouth. Her teeth were like white pearls. It struck him, oddly, that he hoped this girl would never marry, for then she would lose her expressive eyebrows, and she would also blacken her teeth. He quickly amended his wish, for it was cruel to wish a girl to remain unmarried. There was little that life had to offer an unmarried woman.

But now a deep voice rumbled from behind the hedge, and suddenly both he and the girl were silent, listening.

"The Lord of Mito said in his message"—there was the

rustle of paper, and then the man continued—"'There was once a dragon tamed and domesticated that one day drove through wind and cloud in the midst of a hurricane and took flight.'"

"What's that supposed to mean?" Yoshi whispered.

"Your master, Nakahama Manjiro, is like a dragon, I suppose," the girl whispered back. "The Lord of Mito thinks that were he to change his mind and 'fly away' on an American ship, it would be too late to repent."

"Repent what?"

"Letting the man go, who could tell the red-hairs so many secrets."

"What secrets?"

She motioned for him to join her in the garden, where she gave him the broom she was holding and told him to sweep the snow from the stepping-stones while she held back the branches. "At least try to look like you belong here," she said. Then she continued in a low voice, "The shogun, Tokugawa, is in a terrible position. If he admits that his government cannot drive away the barbarians, it is to invite the ruin of the Tokugawa house. The other option, which is to resist, is to invite the destruction of the empire."

"On the one hand, the entire Tokugawa family," Yoshi repeated. "On the other, all of Japan."

"Thus it is whispered everywhere in these halls," the little gardener said softly. "It seems also that the Americans believe the emperor is the supreme leader. They do not understand that the emperor has no power, the shogun is weak and spineless, and the country is run by the Bakufu. The truth is, our country is not strong enough to keep the foreigners out. Our weapons are no better against the outsiders than—than a bamboo sword!"

Yoshi flinched. Had she seen him practicing and was she teasing him? "You shouldn't say such a thing," he said. "It's . . ."

"Treason? It's only what everyone is saying."

"How do you know?"

"Servants hear everything. You should know that. As far as our masters are concerned, we're invisible—it's as if we aren't there. So, in order to hear, all you have to do is keep your ears open . . . *Yoshitaro*. Or should I call you by your nickname . . . *Yoshi*?" Taking the broom out of his hand, she said, "You can call me Kiku." Then she swept her way across a bridge and disappeared behind the snowy shrubs.

Yoshi watched her go, not knowing what to think. How did she know his name? Was this snip of a girl an enemy to watch out for? Or could she be an ally?

Oh, this court of the shogun was a nest of spies! There was no one to trust. And Manjiro—was he a spy, like some of them said? He *was* a strange man, an outsider, like the official had said. Everybody thought so, even the stableboys. Maybe he *was* a spy! Yoshi did not know what to think about anything anymore.

He almost longed for his old job as a sandal bearer. Nothing much to worry about there—except, he reminded himself, Kitsune! It seemed unlikely that rough-mannered Kitsune would ever appear in the shogun's court. Perhaps Yoshi was finally safe from him.

Yoshi thought this while he stared at the place where Kiku had disappeared from view and wondered: Where had she gone? There wasn't anything behind those snowy bushes but a long hedge. But she didn't come back out.

He crossed the bridge and followed her footprints in the snow. Then, glancing around to make sure no one was watching, he stepped behind the bushes.

The girl was nowhere to be seen. Her footprints disappeared at the still-green hedge that separated the garden from—well, whatever it separated it from. She couldn't have gone through the hedge; it was a thick tangle of thorny branches. He certainly wouldn't be willing to try it, at risk of tearing his clothes and skin to shreds.

So where had she gone?

23

LASSOING

Now that the trees were bare of leaves, it was nearly impossible for Yoshi to find a private place to practice with his bamboo sword. He certainly wasn't going to do it anywhere the boys could see him. That would give them more reason to tease him. So instead of the sword, sometimes he practiced throwing a rope the way Manjiro had shown him. Manjiro said that working with the lasso was a good thing to do if you had pondering to do. And Yoshi had pondering to do.

On this late afternoon, the other boys had all led horses to the archery range for practice, and Yoshi found himself alone for a little while. He discovered a warm slice of late afternoon sun outside the stable and spun the loop of rope over his head. And pondered. He pondered if he could rope a sunbeam. He pondered whether he could ever make friends with the other stableboys. But mostly he pondered if he would ever, *ever* earn enough money to pay Ozawa back.

Manjiro had given him a warm quilted jacket and a few coins now and then when Yoshi carried a message or ran an errand for him, and as a stableboy Yoshi got his room and board, but he had earned only a handful of coins for pay.

Feeling the warmth of several pairs of eyes on the back of his head, he turned.

"What are you doing?" Hiko asked, stepping forward into the sunbeam.

Yoshi glanced at the boys. He could say, "Nothing," and ignore them, or he could assume they were really curious and just . . . be nice.

"This," he said, turning to them and holding up the rope, "is called a *lasso*. It's for roping horses or cows."

"Where did you learn that?"

"Manjiro taught me."

"It is another weird barbarian practice," the boy named Enju said.

"How can you work for that outsider?" Hiko stood with arms crossed, watching Yoshi as he pulled the rope in and then looped it carefully.

Han and Shozo began to enumerate Manjiro's faults: He dressed funny. He had strange habits. He smiled too much. He had a funny accent. And after all, he didn't belong at the court of the shogun. He didn't even seem to understand basic rules of etiquette.

"I've heard he takes leftover food home when he eats at restaurants!" Shozo said.

"No, he doesn't!" Yoshi protested.

"Yes," Hiko said. "Everybody says so. How embarrassing!"

"Maybe he shares it with you!" Shozo exclaimed. "You're looking a little chubby!"

All the boys laughed.

Yoshi stalked into the first stall he came to: a new colt's. He busied himself checking the young horse's hooves.

If he had gone along with their teasing, he would have some friends now, he thought. Why *didn't* he just go along with them? Everything they said he had thought himself! And this rumor that Manjiro took his leftovers home when he ate at restaurants—what was to be made of that?

Sometimes Manjiro seemed too unsophisticated and too common for the court of the shogun, where elegance, good breeding, family name, and careful behavior were all-important.

"Why don't I just go along with those boys, since I agree with everything they say?" Yoshi mumbled while he picked bits of straw from the colt's fetlocks.

He heard the boys talking and laughing out there, and he listened as their voices drifted away when they left the stables for their evening meal at the barracks.

The light had grown dim while he'd been in the colt's stall. He puttered around a while longer, making sure the boys were gone before he stole out into the dark evening.

24

EVENING

As he came out into the courtyard, Yoshi noticed a small group of men walking out of the gate and into the street. There was a burst of laughter that he recognized as Manjiro's, and Yoshi instantly realized the men were on their way to have a meal at a restaurant.

Well, Yoshi thought, *I'll follow and watch and see that Manjiro does not take his leftovers, and settle that rumor once and for all!*

Staying far enough behind to not draw suspicion, but close enough to keep track of the group, Yoshi slipped from one shadow to the next. He wouldn't want to have to explain to Manjiro why he was following him.

Manjiro and his friends entered a restaurant, and Yoshi slid into the dark space between two buildings across the street. That way he wouldn't miss seeing Manjiro when he left. From his spot, he had a broad view of the whole street as well as the entrance to the restaurant. He was also quite sure that he himself could not be seen.

He shifted his weight from one foot to the next, trying to stay warm in the crisp winter evening. The air was heavy with the smell of steaming soup and thick strips of eel sizzling on a grill. And . . . hair oil?

The back of his neck prickled. Now he heard voices speaking in low tones, not far away. Some men were conversing secretively in the next entryway!

"How long do we wait?" said one of them.

"Until he comes out," said another.

Were they waiting for Manjiro? Yoshi wondered. Why?

Yoshi pressed himself a little closer to the wall. He didn't dare move, because even the slightest rustle would be enough to alert the men to his presence.

The restaurant door opened and Manjiro's companions stepped out, chattering and laughing. Warm lantern light and the sounds of laughter poured out after them, and then came Manjiro himself. And yes, he was carrying something: a small paper-wrapped package. It must be true what the boys had said.

The noise from across the street prevented Yoshi from hearing all of what the nearby men were saying, but he caught some of their conversation.

"Shall we follow him?" one of them asked.

Yoshi had to work hard to resist the temptation to peek around the corner.

"No. He is with friends," said another voice. "We'll do it another time."

Do *what* another time? Yoshi wondered.

"Meet at the dojo tomorrow—on the other side of the Umaya Bridge—at the hour of the monkey. We can go from there to get something to eat and discuss our plan."

Plan? Yoshi wondered. What sort of plan?

As soon as he heard their retreating footsteps, Yoshi peeked out from around the corner and saw three young samurai of low rank walking away. He was staring after them when one of them glanced back. He quickly ducked into the shadows, but he wasn't sure it had been soon enough. He might have been seen.

When he was sure they were gone, Yoshi followed Manjiro and his friends through snowy streets glowing from the light of the teahouse lanterns.

Near the Ryogoku Bridge, Manjiro stopped when a man approached him.

"It's only a beggar," one of his companions said.

"Why, it is my friend, Baku-san!" Manjiro exclaimed.

Manjiro held out his package from the restaurant and gave it to the man, who bowed and murmured his thanks.

"I am sorry it isn't more," Manjiro said, bowing back.

His companions looked away, embarrassed.

So, Yoshi thought, *that's what he does with the food! He doesn't take it home and eat it—he gives it away to beggars.*

Ryogoku Bridge. (*Ando Hiroshige*)

He didn't know quite what to think. It was not proper to take food from a restaurant. It was even less so to give it away to beggars on the street. If the other boys found out, would they tease Yoshi and his master even more? Or would they see that Manjiro had a kind heart, and that he cared about others?

Yoshi knew what it was like to be hungry. There had been times when he would've been grateful to get anything—the skin of a trout, the dregs from a bowl of soup, an orange peel, or most certainly the leftovers of someone's restaurant meal. Manjiro had been a peasant once, and he'd probably been hungry in his lifetime. He hadn't forgotten what it was like.

So, should Yoshi tell the other stableboys what he knew about the restaurant food? Or not? He struggled with the question for a few moments before realizing that it hardly mattered. There were more important things to think about: Who were those men outside the restaurant, why had they been spying on Manjiro, and what kind of plan were they meeting to discuss?

25

AT THE SOBA SHOP

It was easy to find the dojo near the Umaya Bridge. Yoshi arrived early, sneaked quietly through the gate, and found a shadowy corner in the small front garden from which to watch the samurai arriving. The doors of the dojo were open, and he watched as one of the young men laced on his protective vest and donned his face shield. The student glided onto the smooth wooden floor and took his stance. His hair flowed loosely from behind the mask, and as soon as he and his sparring partner began to fight, Yoshi knew he would not be able to leave. The young samurai was quick. He was graceful. He was relaxed. He moved the way Yoshi wanted to but knew he didn't.

Yoshi watched until the class was over and the group of young swordsmen stepped outside, talking and laughing together. A couple of the voices sounded familiar—were they the men from the previous evening? Although a bit ragged, their clothing was clean, and in spite of their low status, their daisho were well cared for, Yoshi noticed approvingly.

They strode away, the loose-haired one with them, and

Kendo practice. (*Katsushika Hokusai*)

Yoshi followed, listening as bits of their conversation drifted back to him.

"Our divine land is situated at the top of the earth," said one of them. "So says our learned teacher, Aizawa-sensei. The Americans occupy the hindmost region of the earth. Thus its people are stupid and simple."

Yoshi thought that was a fair assessment. He had glimpsed a map of the world in the shogun's palace, and it was true that Japan was right in the center. Its islands were large and, on the map, a deep red color, while other countries took places of lower importance. The place called America was located in an insignificant corner and was an unattractive shade of blue.

"As Aizawa-sensei has told us," the man continued, "all Western countries are like the feet of the world, which trample on other countries."

The young men mumbled their agreement as they entered a soba shop. Yoshi wasn't sure what to do. He wanted to keep listening, but he had no money, so he could hardly go inside and order a bowl of soup. Plus, the man who might have seen him the previous night would likely recognize him, and what would happen then?

He crept alongside the building until he came near a window.

"We must not allow the foreign dogs to defile our country," a deep voice rumbled from within.

"We must resist with the last of our strength," said another voice.

Yoshi felt his heart swell. He was proud there were passionate young samurai who were ready to fight and die to protect their country. He wished he was one of them and not a lowly stableboy. He would join them! He would fight side by side with them!

"If we don't act now, it will be too late," said an authoritative voice. "If we let them in, where will it stop? Not until they have conquered us and taken control of our sacred land. Our country will be overrun with the offal-eating demons!"

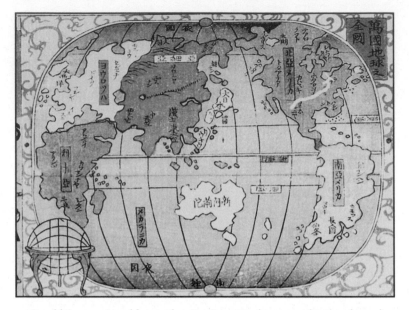

An old Japanese world map showing Japan in the center. (*artist unknown*)

"I didn't know we were going to talk politics," another voice said. "Can't we just relax?"

Yoshi peeked in the window. It was the loose-haired one who'd said that.

"How can you talk of relaxing," a tall, lean one said, "when the barbarians are set to return and either the Bakufu will give in to their demands or there will be war?" The speaker glanced toward the window, and Yoshi ducked.

"The latest edict from the Bakufu . . . ," he heard, then lost the thread of the conversation, picking it up again at "their policy will be to 'evade any definite answer to the barbarian requests, while maintaining a peaceful demeanor.' What good is that supposed to do?"

"So much for our Sei-i Tai-Shogun—Barbarian-Suppressing Great General!" said another voice. "What irony to have a leader so named!"

Yoshi wondered who dared to slander the shogun. He peeked in through the window again.

"Can you suggest another strategy?" It was a rough-looking samurai, definitely in need of a shave, who said this. "Everyone understands that we have no navy and that our coasts are undefended. How do you propose to fight against their warships?"

"We need ships like they have," said the lean one.

"Let's steal one of theirs," the loose-haired samurai said.

"Quit joking," Needs-a-Shave said. "This is a serious matter. Even if you *could* steal one, who would even know what to do with it? How to sail or navigate it?"

Yoshi remembered Manjiro saying that if he had a ship, he could sail it anywhere in the world. He had to bite his tongue to prevent himself from squeaking out the name. *Shh,* he told himself. *You don't know what they'll do if they find you.* He slowly lowered his head.

"Are you suggesting we yield to the demands of the barbarians?" said a soft-voiced bushi. "That is a coward's way, not the way of a true samurai."

"Perhaps we need to think radically about the situation." Yoshi raised his head high enough to see that it was a handsome, serious-faced one who said this. "The country is bound to change. It has to change, whether we allow the foreigners in or not. But *we* must be the ones to make the changes. We must think differently about how we are governed."

"Maybe we should consider the government of the barbarians," the loose-haired samurai suggested.

"Always the jokester," the lean one said.

"That might not be such a far-fetched idea." The serious one's face softened. He even smiled. "I know something about their government. They have something called 'democracy.' Instead of an emperor or shogun, they have a president who is elected by the people. The people also elect the ruling body they call Congress."

"What do you mean 'elect'?"

"The people vote."

"What people vote?"

"Every man gets one vote. You don't have to be a member of a particular family or even to have acquired wealth in order to vote."

"So everyone votes?"

"Well, not everyone. But it is said that anyone who can vote can even become the president!"

"Is this an invention of your imagination?"

"No. I heard all this from Kawada Shoryo. He wrote a book about the man who was a castaway, who went to America and came back."

"Manjiro?" The name slipped off Yoshi's tongue before he had time to think.

All eyes turned toward the window. Yoshi ducked, but not fast enough.

A head leaned out the window. "Who is this little rascal?" the samurai cried, while a big, burly one flew out the door and grabbed Yoshi.

"An eavesdropper! A spy!" the burly one exclaimed, eyeing him up and down. "Let's get rid of him now." The bushi grasped the hilt of his katana but stopped short of drawing it.

"Hold on," said the man in the window. "Bring the boy in here."

The big, bear-like bushi led Yoshi into the restaurant and plunked him down by the low table. Yoshi took a furtive glance at the group before lowering his head. There was the lean one who coughed often, and the one who needed a shave. Another, the one with the soft voice, had a face that reminded him of a catfish, with two long whiskers to match. One stood out as the leader: the serious one, with fire in his eyes. And there was the loose-haired one he'd watched admiringly at his sword practice. Many of them were without crests on their sleeves. That meant they were ronin—masterless samurai.

"Who are you?" the leader demanded to know.

"He smells like a stableboy," the bear-like one said, sniffing.

"And is dressed like one," the lean one said.

A pair of hands pushed a bowl of soup and a set of chopsticks toward Yoshi. "Dozo!" a voice said. "Please!" Yoshi bowed to the hands and to the offered soup.

He stared at the bowl, wondering whether he should or shouldn't eat and what he should or shouldn't say. It was beginning to dawn on him that he might have gotten himself into a terrible predicament.

The serious leader asked, "Is that who you are? A stableboy?"

"Yes," Yoshi said. "But it's not who I *really* am." As soon as he said it, it felt true. It felt right. He wasn't just a stableboy. He wasn't just a sandal bearer. He was more than that. He was a bodyguard, after all. That was his real job, and that was a samurai's job. Therefore, he must *be* a samurai. Right? "It's a disguise," he added. "I am . . . I am bushi, like you." He knew he would have to look them in the face to be convincing. At the thought of it, his insides turned as quivery as bean jelly.

The bear-like one stared at him. "I recognize the little gutter rat," he said. "He works for that man some of us have been watching—the American spy, Nakahama Manjiro."

"He's not American!" Yoshi blurted out, realizing that he'd just confirmed their suspicions.

"And last night he was spying on us," the man continued.

"I wasn't spying on *you*; I was spying on *Manjiro*!"

"Well, which is it?" the leader asked. "Do you work for him or were you spying on him?"

"Both," Yoshi said. "Yes, I work for him. And yes, I was spying on him." He filled his chopsticks full of noodles. One might as well have a last meal, he thought, before one is executed.

"Why were you spying on him?" the leader asked him.

Yoshi was glad his mouth was full. It gave him time to think before speaking. He could hardly tell them that he had been following Manjiro to find out what he did with his restaurant leftovers. That would just make Yoshi seem foolish. He swallowed, slowly thinking through his words, trying to remember the arguments he'd heard at the public bath on the Tokaido. Finally he said, "There are some who believe he is directly responsible for bringing the foreign ships to our shores."

The lean one nodded. "How else can it be explained that the Black Ships came so soon after he returned from the West?"

"The Americans most likely educated him to further their own purpose," the catfish-whiskered one added. "And then sent him in advance of the invading barbarians."

Yoshi nodded and slurped up another big mouthful of buckwheat noodles.

"Obviously," the unshaven one said, "the man who knew all about Western ways, who had lived in America, been educated there, and spoke the language would be called upon to advise the shogun and the Bakufu."

"Ah, but instead of an adviser, what they gain is a spy! A spy for the Americans. Right in the shogun's palace!" The bear-like one slammed his fist on the table.

They all looked at Yoshi, who, not wanting to have to say anything else, lifted the bowl to his lips and took a big mouthful of soup.

"You seem to be of similar mind to us," the leader said to him.

Yoshi nodded, hoping to seem serious and older than he was, which was difficult with his mouth full of noodles.

"Do you agree that the barbarians must be expelled?"

Yoshi nodded wholeheartedly.

"Do you revere the emperor?"

Yoshi nodded enthusiastically.

"Why not join us? Though you are young, you can still serve the country and our cause."

Yoshi wanted to join the cause. To keep the foreigners out and preserve the purity and sacredness of his country. He wanted to be like these men: filled with passion and energy. Men of action! Not like the shogun's advisers, who sat about gnawing their fingernails and endlessly discussing things in hushed voices.

"Would you like an assignment?" the leader of the group asked.

Yoshi could barely murmur, "Yes." Perhaps he would really be considered a samurai. It wasn't so far-fetched. Or maybe he would even be made a samurai. That wasn't impossible, either. After all, Manjiro had been made a samurai. At the thought of Manjiro, Yoshi felt a little pang. Was he betraying his employer?

"You may have a very important role to play in saving our country from the barbarians," the leader said.

The soup in Yoshi's belly seemed to tremble. What would they assign him to do? he wondered. Maybe it would involve carrying a sword. If he had even a short sword, he could help protect the country—and, he reminded himself, he would be a better bodyguard for Manjiro.

"If you do a good job," the man said, "you will be rewarded."

The coughing one held up a coin—a large coin, a gold koban!

It would only take a few of those before he'd have enough money to pay Ozawa back!

"Since you have access to the foreign spy," the leader went on, "we want you to report back to us all that he does and says."

Yoshi stared into his nearly empty soup bowl. It was one thing to spy on Manjiro to find out what he did with his restaurant leftovers, but *this*! This was a *different* kind of spying.

26

YOSHI THE SPY

Yoshi and Manjiro crossed the inner moat and stopped at the first guardhouse on their way to an important meeting with the shogun's councillors. Rumors had spread that the Black Ships could return at any time, and Manjiro had once again been summoned.

The guards glanced at Manjiro's papers, then peered at Yoshi with unusual intensity. At least it seemed that way to him. After many minutes of scrutiny, they were allowed to pass through.

They crossed another bridge, past more guards, through another gate. At every checkpoint, Yoshi's stomach clenched, his muscles tightened. *You are a servant and you are invisible,* he reminded himself. *They are not really noticing you.* But as he and Manjiro traversed the wide gravel yard, which was swarming with armed warriors and sentries, it seemed to Yoshi that every single one of them was eyeing him with suspicion. Even the golden dragons on the castle's gabled rooftops appeared to leer down at him. "Spy!" they seemed to hiss, even though Yoshi had not done any spying yet. It felt as if everyone and everything in the castle suspected that he was at least supposed to be a spy. Everyone, that is, except Manjiro.

Yoshi was accompanying Manjiro as an errand boy or messenger, but it seemed there weren't any errands or messages, so instead Yoshi knelt quietly outside the reception room, trying to concentrate on the conversation within. Mostly, though, he was brooding. He knew what he was supposed to be doing: listening and reporting all that he heard to the samurai at the soba shop. Although he had not reported anything so far, he still felt guilty. Guilty and confused.

What *was* he going to do? If he told the samurai what Manjiro did and said, wouldn't that be betraying his master? And didn't Yoshi owe his loyalty to him? On the other hand, how could it possibly matter if he told them some of the things that Manjiro had told the councillors: that the River of Heaven could be seen in other parts of the world, but in America it was called the Milky Way? Or that thunderstorms occurred in many parts of the world, not just in Japan. Yoshi supposed there'd be no harm in telling the soba shop samurai *that*.

What if he didn't say anything about Manjiro but just reported what the councillors had to say? He could tell them what Lord Ii was saying right now: that without warships, he felt uneasy about pursuing and attacking the Americans.

He could tell them that the Lord of Mito said the

Americans had been watching the country with greedy eyes for years. He said, "They will manage bit by bit to impoverish the country, after which they will treat us just as they like."

It didn't seem as if it would hurt anything to say these things, and then Yoshi could earn the promised coins and be that much closer to repaying Ozawa.

Now Manjiro was insisting that the Americans' intentions were honorable: "It is telling that the motto of the Americans, the phrase they stamp on their currency, is 'E pluribus unum.' It is a Latin phrase that means 'Out of many, one.'"

"And what is that supposed to mean?" one of the councillors asked, echoing Yoshi's own thought.

"It might mean many things," Manjiro replied. "Some think that it means 'Out of many states, one nation.' Or, because the United States is a country of immigrants, 'Out of many nationalities, one people.' Or—"

Yoshi's concentration was broken when he noticed the girl, Kiku, out in the garden. How had she appeared there? He rose and walked over to her. She didn't look at him; instead, she stopped and gazed out, seeming to focus on something far beyond the garden.

"You see?" Kiku said when he reached her. "Even the shogun has to borrow things." She gestured through the opening in the carefully sculpted pines to the view of wooded hills and, beyond them, the distant, misty peak of Fuji-san. "Shakkei, it's called—borrowed scenery. Bringing a faraway view into this very garden, as if part of it."

Yoshi's eyes traveled past the newly budding branches to the distant scene. Beyond the shogun's garden was where everything was happening: Young samurai met in teahouses discussing how the government might be transformed, and foreign ships would soon gather in the bay outside these walls. All the while, a million people held their breath, waiting to see what might happen.

These stone walls and thick hedges could not keep out the world, Yoshi thought. His heart pressed almost painfully against his chest to think of it, but he wasn't sure it was from fear.

Kiku turned to face him and asked, "Have you ever wondered where you belong?"

"No," he answered. It was not his place to wonder such things. But now he couldn't help wondering . . . Where *did* he belong? "Where do you think *you* belong?" he asked. He was surprised how directly they were speaking with each other.

"I don't know . . ." She pointed through the opening in the trees at the faraway view. "Maybe there."

Yoshi remembered his desire to see what lay beyond the dark hills on the far side of the bay. He wanted to tell her about his longing to see more of the world, but he didn't know how to talk about it.

+ + +

Later, sitting in the soba shop, hunched over a bowl of broth, he thought of his conversation with Kiku about belonging. He did not belong here, in this place, with these samurai. He had wanted to belong, had wished that he could be one of them, but he wasn't. And he never would be.

Nonetheless, here is where he was, and the young samurai were peppering him with questions. He was determined not to give them any information about Manjiro, but when they asked what he'd said, he wasn't prepared, and he blurted out, "E pluribus unum."

"What?" said the bear-like one, who was named Kuma. "Now you are speaking gibberish."

The serious one laughed. "It's Latin," he said. "It's a motto of the Americans. I heard about it from Kawada Shoryo, who wrote the book about the castaway. It means"—he paused for a moment, thinking—"'Out of many, one.'"

"And what is that supposed to mean?"

"In America they have many states."

"Thirty-one," Yoshi mumbled around his soup.

"Many states, one nation. I suppose it would be as if our domain lords all worked together to make one unified nation, instead of ruling their domains as if they were kingdoms."

Catfish raised an eyebrow. "I would like to see *that* happen."

"It can mean other things, too," Yoshi said.

The others turned to him. "For instance?"

"America is a nation of immigrants. It could mean 'Out of many nationalities, one people.'"

"They may be all different nationalities, but they are all still barbarians," Coughing One grumbled.

"Or maybe . . ." Yoshi stopped for a moment. Something odd had suddenly occurred to him. "I suppose it *could* mean that out of the many nationalities on earth, we are all still one people."

Kuma snorted. "A little radical in our midst!" he said, and the others laughed.

But the loose-haired one looked at Yoshi thoughtfully. "Is this what your master tells you?" he asked. "That all people are the same?"

Yoshi shoveled more soup into his mouth and stared at the bowl. He was determined not to say anything else about Manjiro, or what he had or hadn't told him.

"That is the founding principle of the United States," the serious one said. "That all men are created equal."

Yoshi expected to hear the rumble of disagreement, but the room was strangely silent. Perhaps, he thought, they were considering the fact that here in their own country, they were all low-level samurai with little power or say in anything.

They had not been born to wealth or power, and so it was unlikely they would ever have either. That is how it was.

Two new young samurai had joined the group, and now one of them spoke. "The thing to do is to go there," he said.

"Go where?" Coughing One asked.

"To America."

The room grew still. After a moment, Catfish said, "Why would you want to do that?"

"Only by learning the barbarians' ways can we hope to defeat them," the young man answered. "Someone must do it. Why not us?"

"How do you propose to get there?"

"We will approach the Americans, explain that we want to go to their country, and ask to be taken aboard one of the ships."

The room filled with murmurs of surprise. "Dangerous!" "Illegal!" "Radical!" the others exclaimed.

"Yes, of course we know that," the self-assured young man said.

Yoshi stared at him open-mouthed.

"If your plan fails . . ." Kuma's voice trailed off.

"We know," the man's companion said. "We are prepared for whatever might happen: arrest, interrogation, even execution. We believe this is the best—the only—course we can take."

The room was silent, everyone considering their words. The only sound was the *sploosh* of a noodle sliding from Yoshi's chopsticks back into the broth.

One day, Yoshi told the men in the soba shop something he knew they would find out anyway. It wasn't a secret. But he could deliver the news a little bit early and thus get some credit for his spy work. Perhaps earn the last bit necessary to make a complete repayment to Ozawa.

"The Black Ships have returned, and there will be a meeting with the barbarians to discuss a treaty," he said.

"They were not supposed to come back for a full year!" Catfish snapped.

Yoshi resisted the urge to shrug—that gesture he'd picked up from Manjiro.

"It is as we feared," Kuma growled. "The Bakufu intends to negotiate with the barbarians."

"There are those of us who think that perhaps an opportunity will arise to prevent the signing of the treaty," Catfish said.

"How do you think you are going to do that?" Loose-Hair asked.

"We do not intend to stand idly by and let our country shame itself in this way," Catfish said. "We intend to . . . do something about the American commodore. Or, if not him, the spy for the Americans—Nakahama—that boy's master." Catfish pointed at Yoshi."Manjiro. He will be there, no doubt."

"What are you suggesting?" Needs-a-Shave asked.

Catfish turned his gaze on Yoshi and said, "Before I speak, the little samurai must go. I don't trust him. If he is willing to tell us what his master says, he is surely willing to report what we say to his master."

There was a rumble of agreement, and Yoshi was escorted out. A coin was plunked in his hand, and he was shooed down the street. He slunk away, wondering what kind of scheme they were hatching, and glad that he hadn't told them everything. He had not told them that Manjiro would *not* be allowed to go to Kanagawa, where the treaty was to be discussed. He had also not told them, since they hadn't asked, that he himself *would* be going. Not officially, of course, but as Manjiro's spy. He looked at the coin in his hand. With this, he finally had enough money to repay Ozawa. Yoshi felt sure that he would find him, for hadn't the engraver said, "Wherever the barbarians are, there you'll find Ozawa"?

Perhaps Yoshi would also be able to find out, when they were all in Kanagawa, what these soba shop samurai were plotting.

PART THREE
WIND

In order to understand yourself you must understand others.

—Miyamoto Musashi, *The Book of Five Rings*

27

JACK ALOFT

Monday, February 13, 1854

Aloft and furl the topsails!" the lieutenant ordered.

Jack grasped a deadeye, hoisted himself up onto the ratlines, and began climbing. He followed Toley, who was behind Willis. Other topmen scrambled up the port-side rigging.

Toley was growling something at Willis, and Jack heard Willis say, "I never did!" after which Toley grabbed Willis's foot and yanked.

"Leave off!" Willis cried, kicking at Toley's hand.

"Avast, Toley!" Jack barked at him. Toley could pull the boy clear off the rigging!

Toley turned his mean-eyed squint on Jack. "This is between me and Willis," he said.

In the meantime, Willis had scrambled up and out of the way.

"Flapjacket!" a mate shouted from below. "What in the name of ginger cake is the snag? Into the top, lad, and sprightly now!"

Toley moved ahead, and Jack followed.

Once the topmen were all aloft and spread out along the yard, Griggs had a word with Jack. "Ye should pick yer fights below—"

"It wasn't my—" Jack started, but Griggs went on.

"You with enough delinquenchies already, what with the marlinspike, the pigs, the tangly lines, and the lost squilgee, too," Griggs added.

It was true. On deck, Jack was a bumbling oaf. He'd dropped a splicing hammer on a midshipman's toes. He'd tumbled down deck ladders, left the pigpen unlatched, and regularly lost his buttons, among other transgressions. But that was on deck.

Aloft was where he excelled. He was quick at climbing the ratlines, and he was fast and sure at casting off gaskets, and reefing sails, too. The first few times he'd gone aloft to loose sails, he'd continually expected to feel himself falling. It was just like in a book he'd been reading about a seafarer who, upon going aloft to loose the skysail, thought, "I seemed all alone; treading the midnight clouds; and every second, expected to find myself falling—falling—falling, as I have felt when the nightmare has been on me." When Jack read that, he'd thought, *That's just how I used to feel.* But not any longer. Now, sometimes, even after his task was done, he'd stay up there, the higher the better.

"Halloo!" came a shout from the deck, and then a call to "clew up the upper topsail."

Jack went to work pulling the lines attached to the sail. But in the middle of it, something caught his eye. He had been so busy with his task that he hadn't looked out until now. So he hadn't seen, rising out of the misty distance, the green hills and gleaming cliffs of white chalk, the tops of precipices, and—seeming to float above all else, as if detached from the rest of the earth—the white-topped cone of Mount Fuji.

Japan! After six months away, they had returned. The commodore had said a year, but he had changed his mind and brought the fleet—eight vessels this time—back to its shores. It was strange, Jack thought, but his heart seemed to lift. Something, maybe the sight of Fuji floating there, as if having nothing anchoring it to earth, made him feel that anything might happen.

The drumroll began, the bosun's whistle twittered, and the shout rang out, "General quarters!"

Jack began his scramble down the rigging. Yes, he thought, something was going to happen. Maybe even something good.

Mount Fuji, seen from the beach. (*Ando Hiroshige*)

28

KANAGAWA

3rd Day of the Month of New Life, 7th Year of Kaei
(March 31, 1854)

The Americans were back. There were the Black Ships, anchored smugly in the bay. And there, emptying from their boats and swarming onto the shore, were the blue-jacketed soldiers. Those jackets fit their hairy bodies so snugly that Yoshi was reminded of white rice tightly rolled into strips of seaweed. It would have been hard to take the soldiers seriously if they weren't also very tall, very large, and every single one with a saber at his side or a musket on his shoulder.

Yoshi elbowed his way through the hundreds and hundreds of curious onlookers, all hoping to catch a glimpse of the strange foreigners. Once through the spectators, he faced a jumble of guards and police, foot soldiers, pikemen, cavalrymen, officers, and the great lords themselves in their painted silk and embroidered brocade. How, he wondered, would he ever find Ozawa in this crowd?

Yoshi's eyes drifted over all these people until finally settling on a row of artists sketching away. And there! The familiar round, bald head with its ring of white hair: Ozawa. For a moment, Yoshi just stood and gazed at the artist who had been so good to him. It seemed like years ago, but it had only been a few months since he'd last seen him.

Ozawa looked up as Yoshi approached.

"You!" the artist exclaimed. "I heard you drowned. Are you a ghost?"

"I did drown," Yoshi answered, "but only for a few moments. I am ashamed to say I let the money go so that I could live. It was a dishonorable act."

"Not at all," Ozawa said. "For had you drowned, the money would have drowned with you. I would have lost my money anyway, and the world would have lost you."

"That would not be so great a loss," Yoshi mumbled.

"Do not say so!" Ozawa said. "You can never know that. Even today you might do a great thing."

Yoshi smiled and shook his head. "I doubt that," he said. "My most humble apologies for the trouble I caused. Please forgive me, Master Ozawa, for all the wrongs I have committed. It was my great honor to serve you. I beg you to accept payment for what I owe you."

Yoshi emptied a pouch full of coins into Ozawa's hands—all he had earned.

"Well!" Ozawa said. "You must have met with good fortune!"

"I am working at the shogun's stables now," Yoshi said.

"Ah!" Ozawa exclaimed. "You see? Your drawings *were* magic." When Yoshi looked at him quizzically, he explained, "Those horses you drew came to life, just like Sesshu's rats!"

Yoshi laughed. "Maybe you are right."

"I have something for you, little bushi." Ozawa presented him with a small drawing kit and some fine rice paper. "You know a samurai needs to be well-rounded. 'The arts of peace in the left hand and the art of war in the right,' so the ancients say."

Somehow, having given away all his money, Yoshi did not feel bad, as he expected he would. In fact, he felt lighter. He had paid his debt, and a great burden had been lifted from his shoulders. He did not think anything could go wrong now.

To fulfill his second obligation, he was to do some spying. Manjiro had been disappointed that he hadn't been asked to interpret during the treaty negotiations. "Oh, to be a fly on the wall!" he'd said, and Yoshi had, a little bit nervously, offered to be that fly.

Now, while everyone else was watching the parade and listening to the strange barbarian music, Yoshi was studying the treaty house. He would hardly be a successful spy if he couldn't hear anything! And he wouldn't be able to hear anything unless he got inside. But how was he going to do that?

He watched as the officials entered the building. Those outside began to mill about, or sat under the trees to picnic on hot rice crackers and steamed buns.

Yoshi crept around to the back of the treaty house. Even from the outside, he could tell that the building had a raised floor—he supposed so the Japanese officials could sit up there and—

He stopped in mid-thought. The elevated floor was probably hollow underneath. He casually tapped at it with the side of his foot. Yes, it *was* hollow, and there was a loose board, too!

No one was looking. Now was the time. He ducked down, squeezed through the opening, and, using his elbows to propel himself, scooted along the ground under the floor.

The sound of muffled voices and thumping feet came from overhead. And—he stopped for a moment—was that . . . breathing?

He began to have the distinct feeling that he was not alone under this floor.

As his eyes adjusted to the gloom, he made out several pairs of glittering eyes . . . ten prone bodies . . . and ten dully gleaming katanas.

29

GIFTS

From the American government to the Emperor, the Empress, to various heads of state, and to the Japanese people:

Miniature working railroad

High-pressure firefighting hose and apparatus

Magnetic telegraph

Daguerreotype apparatus

Copper-clad lifeboat and copper-clad surfboat

Audubon's *Birds of America*

Colt six-shooters, Hall's rifles, Maynard's muskets, cavalry swords, army pistols, carbines, cartridge boxes and belts

Wagons, boats

Agricultural implements

Several casks of whiskey, cases of champagne, bottles of cordial

Perfumery

Telescope

Boxes of tea

Baskets of Irish potatoes

From the Emperor to the President of the United States, to Commodore Perry, and to the squadron:

Lacquered ware: gold lacquered writing apparatus, boxes, bookcase, writing tables, notepaper, and letter paper

Assorted seashells

Silks, pongee, crepe

Porcelain

Fans

Umbrellas

Tobacco pipes

35 bundles of oak charcoal

200 bags of rice

4 small dogs

A couple of tailless cats

500 chickens

30

THE LARK

Friday, March 31, 1854

Jack lingered near a group of officers who were smoking their pipes and drinking from small cups of tea that had been passed around to those waiting outside the treaty house. He listened with one ear to their conversation and with the other to the calls of birds drifting down the hill from the forest's edge.

The officers were discussing the reaction of the Japanese to the American gifts, which were on impressive display along the waterfront: a working telegraph, a high-pressure firefighting hose and apparatus, and a complete miniature railroad, whose cars ran around an eighteen-inch track for a full 350 feet.

"The little train went scudding round and round like a Shetland pony," one of the officers exclaimed, "causing much wonder and astonishment."

The firefighting hose, too, apparently caused quite some hilarity when its high-pressure stream of water hit the crowd and, Lieutenant Preble remarked, "knocked them into a heap!"

The conversation then turned to the gifts from the Japanese and discussion of the giant Japanese wrestlers who had carried the two hundred bales of rice, each bale weighing at least 125 pounds.

"One of those giants carried a sack suspended by his teeth!" Mr. Allen said. "Another took a sack in his arms and turned repeated somersaults as he held it."

The officers spoke of silks and crepes and pongee (whatever that was!), writing desks and writing paper, seashells, lacquered ware, umbrellas, dolls, and fans.

Sumo wrestlers displaying their strength by carrying rice. (*artist unknown*)

"Fans!" Mr. Williams sniffed.

"When exhibited in the U.S., I think, these presents will prove a great disappointment," said Lieutenant Preble. "They form a pretty display, but I should judge of not much value. Their gifts to us are not worth over a thousand dollars. I am sure one of our gifts to them, say, Audubon's *Birds of America*, is worth more than everything given to us. And our miniature railroad engine and car cost several times their value."

"Do you suppose it is due to their ignorance of the cost of things given them, and therefore their inability to judge what would be of corresponding value?" Mr. Allen asked.

"Or is it owing to their petty character?" Mr. Williams mumbled around his pipe. He was having trouble getting it lit, and Lieutenant Preble passed Jack a box of matches, indicating that he should help the gentleman with a light.

Jack scratched a match to flame and lit Mr. Williams's pipe while the lieutenant continued. "Even the commodore remarked on the meager display," he said.

"Well, at least our expedition has fared well," Mr. Wells said. "Not a shot was fired, not a man wounded, and not a piece of property destroyed. Certainly, we have left a favorable impression."

"Aye," agreed the purser. "The Americans and Japanese will soon be on lasting terms of friendship with each other, I have no doubt."

Jack wondered about that. It seemed an odd sort of friendship when you anchored your ship broadside so as to aim your cannon at your "friends." Or to arrive with your marines with their rifles bayoneted and bristling like so many quills on a porcupine. The Japanese hadn't looked particularly friendly, either, with their mounted archers and pike bearers and every man with his swords in his sash.

He wasn't sure he would call this "friendship," unless you could bully someone into being your friend.

"Oh, I almost forgot, Flapjacket," Lieutenant Preble said, reaching into his pocket and passing Jack a piece of paper. "Will you pass this note to Lieutenant Bent?"

Jack took the offered note, put it in his pocket, and started off to the treaty house. He stopped when he saw Toley striding toward him, hands in his pockets and wearing a crooked grin. That grin made Jack wary. He considered making a run for it, but he had the message to deliver, so he strode on.

"Flapjacket!" Toley bellowed. "I've been looking for you. Me and Willis are going to see if we can't filch one of them swords."

"You're crazier than a bedbug!" Jack said. "Do you have any idea how much trouble—"

"I'm not talking about *stealin'* it," Toley said, stepping into stride with Jack. "We'll barter for it. We'll trade it for . . . I dunno."

"Is this something Willis wants to do?" Jack asked.

"'Course he does."

"Bet he doesn't," Jack said.

"Why would he agree, then?" Toley said.

Jack stopped and looked at Toley. "Are you telling me you really don't know? You bully him into agreeing with you. If he doesn't go along with you, you make his life miserable."

"Naw," Toley said. "Willis—he's my pal."

"He is not your pal," Jack said. "He's just afraid of you, that's all. That's not a friendship." Toley narrowed his eyes—whether in anger or consternation, Jack couldn't tell. "Why don't you just . . . I don't know . . . ," Jack continued, "try being nice to him, if you want him to like you. Or if 'nice' is too far out of your range, just be decent. Why don't you *ask* him what he wants to do, instead of *telling* him what he wants to do?"

Jack supposed he'd now brought the wrath of Toley upon his own head, but he didn't want to wait to find out. He took a left turn and stalked out into a field.

"Where are you going?" Toley called after him.

Jack spun around. "It's no business of yours. Good-bye and good riddance." He strode purposely into the wheat fields surrounding the grounds, as if he had a plan. Toley didn't follow.

The day was so fine and the air so clear, Jack soon forgot

the sour feeling he'd gotten from Toley. The wheat was greening, just as he supposed it was back at his family's farm, and when a lark burst out of the tender stalks and took wing, Jack felt his heart lift. Trilling and warbling, the lark was like a voice from home.

Jack watched the bird as it flew the length of the field and into the forest beyond. The forest—that's where he wanted to go! The smell of it rushed down the slope to greet him: the scent of green growing things, the peppery scent of ferns, and tantalizing unfamiliar smells, too. He would like to be among trees again. Like at home, when he went into the forest to hunt grouse with only a stone or two instead of a fowling piece.

He climbed the hillside and found a path that led into the forest. Under the tall trees, the ground was speckled with shadow and light as the branches overhead bent in the wind. As he went farther into the forest, the hum and bustle of the crowds grew distant, and eventually disappeared altogether. Toley, too, seemed far away and almost long ago, as if he were someone Jack had known some other time. Soon there was only the burble of water, the sound of the breeze tangled in the tops of the pines, and a multitude of singing insects to keep him company.

Jack felt drawn forward, through giant ferns and dark glens, along a rushing brook, over mossy ground, past swarms of glittering butterflies, under huge trees circled with tasseled rope, past red-painted arches and small shrines tucked into rock walls, as well as strange stone statues lined up like rows of orphans waiting for their supper. And here and there, half hidden among the grass and weeds, a stone Buddha silently watched his progress.

The urge to see what lay beyond the next bend or over the next rise had always been strong in him, but now there was something else drawing him forward, as if the trilling of insects, the crying of birds, the whispers of leaves all urged him to some place he must go.

The deeper he went, the taller the trees and the darker the forest. Except for the rush of water and the warbling of birds, it was quiet. He felt as if he had stepped into another world, a world outside of time.

The silence seemed deep and meaningful; it told of centuries of stillness and contemplation, of moss growing and water dripping and leaves fluttering, the fronds of ferns unfurling, of a people moving with the tempo of this ancient forest and its ancient ways.

He had no business here, he thought, out of place as he was. As out of place as the Americans were in this whole country, really.

He began to doubt everything he thought he knew.

Should he be here? Should the *Americans* be here? *Were* there Americans here, clustered in great numbers on the waterfront? *Were* there ships in the bay? *Had* he just heard a lark singing in just the same way larks sang at home? *Did* he have a home in America? Was there even such a place as America?

No, all of that was gone, and all that existed was this ancient forest, old as that white-peaked mountain—the one called Fuji-san—old as the earth itself.

Eventually, he knew, a cloud would scud by and blot out the light that made the butterflies glitter; a gust of wind would spoil the stillness. The magic of the moment would end, and then he would finally have to admit what he had been trying to ignore: that he had become completely and utterly lost.

But he wouldn't think about that right now. He would just stand and listen to the brook, chattering along just as brooks at home did, except that this brook sounded distinctly Japanese.

Then he realized that what he heard was not the chattering of water running over stones, but voices. Actual human voices. Voices speaking Japanese. Angry, dangerous-sounding Japanese. Although he couldn't understand the words, he did understand the tone, and it made the fine hairs on the back of his neck stand up.

In a few steps, he reached the top of a rise, where he looked down into a glen, and in the clearing stood a cluster of armed warriors, two of them pointing spear-like weapons at an unarmed boy.

That boy! Jack thought. *Isn't that the same boy . . . ?* The same boy he'd locked eyes with in July—the artist's assistant.

Just walk away, Jack said to himself, as he slowly stooped to pick up a fist-sized rock. *This is not your problem. You don't know anything about it. Just leave these people to deal with their own problems.* He picked up another. *You might only make it worse. What if the boy has committed some horrible crime? You have no idea what is going on, so just leave it alone.*

But it was almost as if he looked at his mirror image: a boy at the opposite end of the world who seemed to get into the same—well, maybe even worse—trouble than Jack Sullivan.

31

ANGRY RONIN

Right now, Yoshi thought, between a brush and a sword, he would take a sword any day. Unless he could *paint* a katana that would then spring into his hand, a brush was not going to help him out of his predicament.

If, however, he had a daisho right now, he might be able to get all four of the men who surrounded him, two of whom—Kuma and Catfish—he knew. He would have to use his short sword to make it work, but then he could do it: First he'd make a backward thrust with his wakizashi to the abdomen of the pikeman behind him while at the same time drawing his katana. With that, he'd make a large, circular overhand slice, catching the man to his right in the neck, and the next one across the middle. That would leave just one remaining bushi, and the two of them would have to fight it out.

"He's just a peasant," the pikeman was saying. "We should get rid of him now and forget about it. Why are we bothering with him?"

"He's only a boy. We should let him go," said another samurai.

"No," said Kuma. "Kitsune will be here soon. Kitsune will know what to do with him."

Yoshi's head jerked up. *Kitsune?*

The familiar *thud thud thud* of his footsteps announced the man's approach, and Yoshi squeezed his eyes shut. *If only I could disappear right now,* he thought. *If only I could exhale my soul like the Chinese immortal, Tekkai, and in this way travel wherever I wanted, without my cumbersome body to lug around.* But that was as likely as sailing away on one of the Black Ships.

Maybe it would be a different Kitsune, Yoshi thought. He opened his eyes. No. It was the Kitsune he knew, glaring down at him, his face flushed with anger, except for the pale, livid scar that ran down one side of his face.

"You!" Kitsune stopped abruptly and turned to the others. "This is a little troublemaker! Where did you turn him up?"

"He crawled under the treaty house floor," one of the men said, "where some of our men were hidden."

"We know him from Edo, where we thought he was spying on us, but he was spying on the outsider, Nakahama," Catfish said. "Or so he claims."

"He claims a lot of things," Kuma added. "He says that he wants to join us. He claims to be a bushi disguised as a stableboy."

"And you believed that nonsense?" Kitsune asked.

"No, of course not," Kuma said. "But we thought he might be useful, since he had a connection to the American spy."

"Yes . . . ," Kitsune said, drawing out the word. "That is true. Very true." He bent down and breathed impolitely in Yoshi's face. "Well, little samurai, although you have weaseled away from me twice, there will not be a third time. Perhaps it would be to your benefit to tell us where we might find the American spy."

"He isn't here! Did you think the shogun would trust him to come here?"

"Oh, so you are doing his spying for him? You are perhaps to meet with the foreign devils and tell them secrets?"

"No," Yoshi said. "What nonsense!"

A loud crash in the brush startled everyone.

"What was that?" said the man with the pike.

"You, you, and you, go take a look," Kitsune said, pointing to three of the others and indicating that he and Catfish would stay to guard their troublemaker.

The three bushi went off to investigate. But as soon as they were gone, pebbles and stones began to cascade down the incline from the opposite direction. Yoshi and the two remaining samurai glanced that way to see a red-hair—an actual red-haired boy—clamoring into the glen.

Before Kitsune or Catfish had time to react, the red-hair had clipped Catfish in the forehead with a rock, bringing him to his knees.

Kitsune moved toward the boy, his katana drawn.

What was happening? Yoshi wondered. Had this little barbarian blundered his way into their midst, or was he trying to *help* Yoshi? Why would a barbarian do that? It made no sense. On the other hand, it appeared there was an opportunity to escape, especially since Kitsune was going after the American boy, leaving Yoshi free to make a run for it.

But did he have an obligation to help the boy? Yoshi wondered. Certainly, if the boy had been Japanese, Yoshi would owe him his life, and thus his gratitude. But this was a barbarian boy, so he wasn't sure.

Kitsune was closing in. If Yoshi didn't do something, the red-hair would be cut down. The boy looked up, and Yoshi recognized him—it was that boy, the same boy who'd smiled at him the previous summer. Before he could think any more about anything, Yoshi flung himself across the space, landing squarely on Kitsune's back. The big bushi came down hard, his katana clanging against the rocky ground.

As Kitsune struggled to rise, Yoshi took off running, the other boy with him.

◆ ◆ ◆

The forest was a green blur as they skidded and skittered down slopes, dodging trees and roots, skirting boulders, racing through lush ferns and among giant trees, up and down hillocks, over rocky ground and soft moss.

Shouts echoed through the forest. Glancing over his shoulder, Jack saw not one or two but five angry warriors bearing down on them. "Jack Sullivan," his mother had always said, "trouble follows you." *Here comes trouble*, he thought.

Looking ahead, he noticed a grove of thickly growing bamboo, and he watched as the Japanese boy slid between the slender trunks, then wove among them until he disappeared from view. *I'd better follow*, Jack thought, *before I lose track of the boy.*

It was a strange and eerie place to be, among these tall, thin trunks. Jack kept his eyes on the Japanese boy and tried to keep up. Any sound they made was covered by the clattering of the stalks in the wind and the rustling of leaves. But after a time, these sounds were overpowered by the roar of a river or maybe a waterfall. A sound that grew louder and louder as they made their way through the bamboo. Now, Jack was quite sure, he and the other boy could not be seen or heard.

But when they stepped out of the bamboo forest, it only took a heartbeat to see they were not out of danger. To the sides were impenetrable thickets, a tangle of brambles. Ahead of them lay a deep chasm. And below them surged a river, roiling and foaming. Over the roar of the water drifted the sharp voices of the angry samurai, who were making their way through the bamboo. It was either turn around and go back toward the shouting warriors or—somehow—go forward.

32

OVER THE PRECIPICE

N

ot far from where they stood, Jack noticed that a large
tree had fallen in such a way that it spanned the canyon.
The distance from it to the river below was no greater than
that of the upper topsail to the deck, he judged, and it was
wider and thicker than a yard.

There was no point in hesitating, and Jack dashed out
onto it. He was nearly across when he thought to look back.
The Japanese boy stood as if paralyzed at the edge of the
ravine, having taken not one step out onto the fallen tree.
He had a stricken look on his face that Jack recognized. In
fact, Jack was quite sure he had worn the same expression
the first time he'd been told to run aloft and loose the
topgallants.

Behind the boy, crashing through the bamboo, came the
warriors.

Jack gestured to the boy to come toward him, but in
spite of the approaching warriors, the boy seemed rooted to
the spot. Reminding himself that he'd done this a hundred
times on skinnier timbers, Jack turned carefully around,

made his way back to the frightened boy, and held out his hand.

Yoshi wondered—did the red-hair want him to walk out on that fallen tree? When he hesitated, the boy grabbed hold of his hand and started walking backward on the log, feeling with his feet, while pulling Yoshi along with him.

Yoshi kept his eyes on the red-haired boy's face, making sure not to look down. It didn't matter whether he could see or not, though; he could hear the roar of the river below and sense the void beneath him.

When he finally stepped off the log onto solid earth, Yoshi would have liked to collapse in a heap on the ground. But the foreign boy was chattering, urging Yoshi to help as he pushed and shoved at the tree trunk. When Yoshi finally understood what the boy was trying to do, he, too, put his back against the heavy trunk and pushed. The log creaked, groaned, and, just as their pursuers reached the edge of the ravine, let go.

As he watched the tree plunge down and down to the river below, Yoshi's stomach flipped and turned. The American boy was already running, and Yoshi intended to follow. But something shiny in the dirt caught his eye. *Button*, he remembered Manjiro calling it, as he tucked the small item into his sleeve. Then he scrambled after the red-haired boy, glancing only once behind him to see the startled and angry faces of the samurai standing on the other side, at the cliff's edge.

Down they flew, under the tall trees, with the foaming river crashing and booming below, then over a wooden bridge and through the green mist into forests fragrant with pale white blossoms.

Soon Yoshi began to catch tantalizing glimpses of the glittering bay through the trees. And in the bay, the Black Ships.

Maybe his head was a little light from the exertion, because for a moment he imagined himself on the deck of one of those ships. He imagined how it would feel to be pushed along by sails or steam, the mighty ship cleaving the water with such force and speed that it left a foaming wake behind. His heart lifted to think of it. He could imagine the coastline of Japan receding, becoming smaller and smaller, while the vast ocean loomed ahead.

But no. That could never happen. Here is where they would part, Yoshi knew. He was grateful to the boy for saving his life, but now he would be happy to be rid of him. The boy would go back to the treaty grounds, and from there to the boats that would take him to his ship.

As for Yoshi, he planned to stay hidden in the forest until dark and then cautiously make his way back to Edo. And then his life would go back to the way it had been before.

The boys lurched to a halt at the wooded edge of the farmer's-field-turned-treaty-area, with Jack grabbing a tree to stop himself. Beyond the trees and past the field, he could see the makeshift buildings, and beyond that the sparkling water in the bay, and in the bay the ships. What he did *not* see were the crowds, the rows of blue-jacketed sailors, or the boats lined up along the shore. His heart, already pounding from the hard run, throbbed. There must be at least *one* boat still ashore—*mustn't* there? One they couldn't see, perhaps?

Yoshi also took in the scene. Maybe, he thought, there would be a Japanese boatman who would take the boy to his ship. He peeked out from the trees, looking behind and all around them. Seeing no one, he signaled to the American to follow him, and the two of them darted out from the forest and streaked across the field until they reached the water's edge.

What they found was not only that the American boats had departed but that the ferryboats were gone, too. The last one was just disappearing into the twilight haze.

An old man stood staring out at the Black Ships, watching as the lanterns were lit, one by one, so the ships began to twinkle with light. An occasional strain of music drifted over the water.

"Grandfather," Yoshi addressed him. "Do you know if there is a boatman?"

"All gone," the old man answered, trying hard not to stare at the red-haired boy.

The two boys continued along the shore until they came to a group of fishermen huddled around a small bonfire on the beach, their boats pulled up on shore nearby.

"The barbarians left one of their people behind," Yoshi told the fishermen. "Will one of you take him back to the ships?" He pointed out to the bay, which was growing darker.

Boats in the bay. (*Ando Hiroshige*)

The fishermen looked at the ground, their feet, anywhere but at the boys. No one said anything. One of the fishermen stuck a straw into the fire and touched the burning straw to his pipe and puffed. "It is forbidden to approach the ships," he said, drawing on his pipe, "unless you are an official boat with official permission."

Even if it wasn't forbidden, another one said, who knew what the barbarians would do to you if you drew too close?

"They'll send someone from the Black Ships for him once they know he's missing," suggested the fisherman. "He should just wait here on the waterfront." He reached into his boat and pulled out a basket full of oranges and held it out to the boys. "Dozo," he said. "Please, help yourself."

Yoshi thanked the man and took a handful of oranges, wondering if he should leave the boy at the waterfront, as the fisherman suggested. But what would those bushi do to the boy if they laid hands on him? Would they dare to harm him? Yoshi wasn't sure about the others, but he felt certain that, given the chance, Kitsune wouldn't hesitate to lop off a head or two. If it was an American head, so much the better. That's probably what that group of bushi had been plotting to do anyway, before Yoshi had crawled under the treaty house floor and disrupted their plans.

While Yoshi was thus in thought, he glanced at the boy. Jack had helped himself to some oranges, and now the fishermen were clustered around him, examining the buttons on his jacket. Yoshi's eyes traveled beyond them and up into the hills, where he noticed movement—and then, suddenly, like a flock of crows, their kimono sleeves flapping like wings, the five bushi swept down out of the hills.

Yoshi grabbed the boy's arm and ran, first down the beach and then, as soon as he could, plunging off into the forest and once again into the hills. When the boys stopped to catch their breath, they crouched behind a big boulder and looked back toward the waterfront. For a moment, there was no sign of their pursuers, but then they appeared from behind the trees, approaching the same fishermen, who waved their arms vaguely toward the forest.

The five samurai all turned and squinted into the trees, then fanned out, moving up the hill toward the boys.

PART FOUR
FIRE

In selecting a position for yourself, we speak of "carrying the sun on your back," that is, facing your enemy with the sun behind you.

—Miyamoto Musashi, *The Book of Five Rings*

33

CARRYING FIRE ON YOUR BACK

The sun was low in the western sky, and shafts of golden light pierced the forest. Rather than sticking to the shadows, Yoshi guided the foreign boy along the corridors of brilliant light. They often had to hold a hand over their eyes to see their footing. Yoshi knew that their pursuers would also have a hard time seeing the two boys who ran ahead of them.

Yoshi led them west, toward the setting sun but away from the bay. He knew that he should be thinking about how to get the boy back to his ship, but right now every fiber of his being was focused on staying out of the reach of those bushi.

The twinkling lights of the ships receded behind them. The strains of fiddle music faded. Why, Jack wondered, were they moving farther and farther away from the bay? And they just kept moving away—crashing through brush, fording streams, clambering up and down hillsides.

Finally the boys stopped for a moment and listened. They could not hear the sounds of pursuers. No thudding footfalls. No clatter of stones. No distant voices.

Yoshi realized how raw his throat had become from breathing so hard. He reached into his sleeve and pulled out an orange.

"Dozo," he said, offering it to Jack.

"No, thanks," Jack said. His pockets bulged with his own oranges. But even though he knew he must be hungry, he didn't think he could eat.

In the still evening, a bird called out a single sad note. The bird seemed to echo Jack's sad thoughts. Surely there'd be someone from the *Susquehanna* who would go ashore asking after him, wouldn't there? Sailors were constantly going ashore to deliver this or that . . . but maybe not anymore. The treaty had been signed, the gifts had been delivered and received, the surveys had been conducted. Perhaps everything was finished and the fleet would weigh anchor and move to wherever the commodore said to go next.

Jack's empty stomach felt emptier. His whole insides felt empty. What if . . . what if the fleet just left without him? He was, after all, only a lowly cabin boy, a troublesome boy at that, who, for all his shipmates knew, might have just run way. He certainly wouldn't be the first sailor to jump ship. Why should they wait or even look for him?

He thought of how Toley would tell them that Jack had said "Good-bye and good riddance" before he stalked off into the forest. He squeezed his eyes shut. He supposed Toley would want to get back at him for the things he said. What better way than to see Jack abandoned in Japan?

His stomach rumbled insistently, and he reached into his pocket for an orange, but there was such an ache in the back of his throat, he wasn't sure he'd be able to swallow. He peeled the orange and bit into it, hoping it would be bitter, that its sourness would keep him from crying. But the first juicy burst of flavor was so sweet and delicious that he felt the tears come and his nose begin to run.

Jack didn't want to cry in front of the Japanese boy, and he reached into his other pocket for a handkerchief. Instead, his hand brushed against a piece of paper. He pulled it out and unfolded. It was the note Lieutenant Preble had given him back at the treaty grounds, the one he was supposed to deliver to Lieutenant Bent. He wiped his nose with the back of his hand and squinted at it, but it was too dark to read Preble's faint scrawl. Ah, but wait. Didn't he also have the officer's box of matches?

Jack fished the matches out of another pocket and, holding the paper up where he could see it, struck a light.

A gasp from the Japanese boy made Jack look up.

That was a wonder, Yoshi thought, a stick that lit like that! If Yoshi had wanted to make fire, he would have needed flint

A Three Stars matchbox.

and steel. The American boy handed the box to him, and Yoshi slid it open and examined the little sticks within, then squinted at the cover: a picture of three red stars in a row. He handed the box back to the American.

Jack could just make out the writing on the note by the light of the match: The message said all officers were to wear full-dress uniforms for the banquet to be given by the Japanese commissioners in their honor. That was to be in two days.

Hope surged! A party on shore in two days! Jack leaped up and did a little jig. "Party!" he exclaimed. "On shore! Banquet. Bang-*quet*. You savvy?" He had to make the boy understand! He had to get back in time for the party! American boats were certain to be onshore then.

Jack gathered up a few twigs and sticks and got a little campfire going. Then he stood up, and in the glow of the fire pointed to himself and said, "Jack."

"Jack," Yoshi repeated, and inclined his head in a little bow of acknowledgment. He pointed to himself and said, "Yoshitaro." When Jack stumbled on the name, Yoshi offered his nickname, "Yoshi."

"Yoshi," Jack repeated. He had made up his mind, though. He was not, under any circumstances, going to *bow*. So he stuck out his hand.

Yoshi stared at the hand for a moment and then remembered that was how the barbarians greeted one another, so he extended his arm and they shook hands. It was a strange custom, Yoshi thought. Afterward he had to resist the impulse to wipe his hand off on his kimono.

Then Jack handed Yoshi the note. Yoshi stared at it and was reminded of a poem he had heard about the way Dutchmen wrote:

Dutch letters
Running sideways
Are like a line of wild geese
Flying in the sky.

That is what the English writing looked like, too, flapping its wings across the page. He gave the note back to Jack.

Jack held up the paper, pointed at it, and began to

pantomime things. He pointed in the direction they had come—toward the bay, Yoshi assumed. Then he pretended to eat. Then drink. Then he wove around loopily, like he'd had too much sake to drink. He leaped and hopped about. Maybe it was supposed to be dancing? In the flickering firelight, his antics took on a strange stop-and-go quality, fading in and out in a mesmerizing way. Yoshi leaned in, watching, laughing, and wondering what crazy thing that boy would do next.

Jack juggled oranges; he did some funny dances; he stood on his head; and finally he sighed and plopped down, worn out.

That kid had really been enjoying the show, Jack thought. His brown face glowed in the firelight, and he laughed a little too often, as far as Jack was concerned—what was so funny? Jack surely hoped Yoshi had understood his pantomime, because he did not want to live out his days in Japan, which, if those crazy warriors caught up with them, might not number very many!

He threw a few more sticks on the fire and tried to make himself comfortable on the cold ground. He never thought he would long for his hammock in the stuffy tween decks, but he did now. He'd even happily share his hammock with Toley's stinky boots and stockings, if only he could be back in the ship, safe and sound.

❖ ❖ ❖

At first Yoshi sat, alert for any snap of twig, rustle of leaves, whisper of fabric. But the only sound was the crackling of their little fire, and beyond that, the trilling, ticking, buzzing, and humming of a million nighttime insects. And the heavy, sleeping breathing of the American boy named Jack.

Yoshi could easily just walk away now. If he walked through the night, he would be back at the stables in time for work, and life would resume as before. Except that he knew it would not.

He looked up at the small patches of sky he could see between the branches, where a few stars quivered in the darkness. Everything moved, he'd heard it said: The earth, the heavenly bodies in the vast sky—it all turned, slowly revolving. It made him dizzy to think of it. If even the stars could not stand still—if even the very earth must spin—then how did he expect anything, his life included, to remain in one place?

His life—nobody's life—would ever be the same again. He felt it the way he felt the trembling of the stars and the movement of the earth: in his very bones.

He knew he would help the boy, Jack. But since he couldn't risk waiting at the waterfront, he needed someone who could help Jack get back to his ship. But whom could he trust?

Manjiro, he thought. Manjiro would know what to do, and he could speak the barbarian's tongue. But that meant Yoshi would have to get Jack all the way to Edo. And Edo was a sacred city, forbidden to all outsiders. Hadn't Ozawa told him how the officials had threatened to commit seppuku if Perry took his steamships there? If Yoshi were to take Jack to Edo, he would have to smuggle him in. If he was going to be smuggled, that meant Jack would need a disguise.

Where and how was he going to get that? Yoshi had given all his money to Ozawa. He didn't regret that, but now he had no money with which to buy clothes for Jack. In a pouch tied to his waist sash was the drawing kit and fine rice paper that Ozawa had given him. He could trade that, he supposed. But the thought of losing the gift from Ozawa so soon made him almost unbearably sad. Maybe, instead of selling it, he could draw some pictures to trade. That's what he would do at first light, he decided. That is, Yoshi thought as he finally closed his eyes, if he was still alive.

34

THE DIGUISE

Yoshi awoke just before dawn. Light the color of lotus blossoms filtered through the trees. He looked around, wary, in case he had awakened only to find those bushi staring at him. But there was just the slumped, sleeping form of the barbarian boy, the quiet of the forest, and the birds flitting among the leaves.

He rose, walked to a nearby stream, drank, shed his clothes, and took a chilly bath. Although it was now past "the hour that the gods bathe," it was not far from it. The icy water shook him free of sleep and, he tried to convince himself, fear.

He slid into his clothing and put a little water in the inkwell, then carried his drawing kit back to where he'd been sitting. He pulled the brush from its place and the paper from his sleeve and set these things before him.

What should he paint?, he wondered. A horse? A sword? A barbarian? He didn't have a live horse as a model. He didn't have a real sword to try to copy. But he did have a barbarian, right there, fast asleep. And more than anything else, people loved pictures of barbarians.

Yoshi started drawing. He tried to make the drawing as lifelike as possible, but he remembered that his previous customers had complained if he didn't make the noses or ears big enough. They said his barbarians weren't as hairy as they should be or as misshapen. Some said they'd seen pictures of barbarians with only one eye or with holes in their chests or with arms that dragged on the ground. He wasn't going to go that far, but he added a little length to Jack's nose and some floppy earlobes. He put more hair on his head, and some on his face, too. He drew a few more pictures, embellishing and exaggerating a little more each time.

While he drew, he examined Jack very closely. Fortunately, the boy's eyes were closed. Otherwise, Yoshi would never have dared scrutinize him this way. Jack's skin was very fair. Small flecks of color dotted his face. The way his hair caught the light made it almost look like burning coals, as if his whole head might flame up at any moment. The locks of his hair bent this way and that, like waves on a stormy sea.

The more he studied the boy's face, the more, well, normal it became. Yoshi even got used to his speckled skin. He wasn't a *terrible*-looking person. Not *completely*.

Last drawing, Yoshi thought, setting brush to paper. Then it would be time to go. He glanced up one more time—this time into Jack's open eyes, which so startled him, he dropped his brush. He fumbled on the ground trying to find it.

"What are you doing?" Jack said, sitting upright and peering over at the pictures. "Is that supposed to be me?" He laughed. "I don't look like that! For one thing, do I have a beard?" He stroked his chin and looked at Yoshi.

Yoshi didn't understand the words, but he understood that Jack was complaining. How could Yoshi explain that maybe it wasn't an exact drawing but it was the kind of image that people expected—and wanted—to see? He couldn't. Maybe now was the time to try that thing with the eye that Manjiro did. He closed one eye and opened it again, then looked at Jack to see his reaction.

Jack squinted at him. "Something wrong with your eyes? Is that it?" he said. "You need to take some drawing lessons, buster."

"Time to go," Yoshi said, motioning for Jack to follow him. They started off, wending their way downhill, then stopped in a cemetery on a wooded hill above a temple grounds. The cemetery seemed untended and a little forgotten, a good place to leave Jack while Yoshi found someone with whom to do a little bartering.

Yoshi gestured to Jack to stay behind the gravestone, and to *stay down!*

So Jack hunkered down behind the stone. He'd slept fitfully, his stomach was empty, and he was not at all sure if Yoshi would come back. On top of that, he supposed those crazy warriors could show up at any moment. *Well,* he thought, *there's no use feeling sorry for myself. I wanted an adventure, and I got one.*

Every little chirp, snap, or rustle made his nerves tingle, and he kept himself hidden as well as he could. He kept expecting those crazy Japanese desperadoes to come through the cemetery where he was hidden, swinging their long swords through the tall grass.

The day was so quiet that he could hear the patter of slippered feet on paving stones and the crunch of footfalls on gravel. Voices drifted to him: People who knew each other, perhaps saw each other every day, greeting one another in familiar tones. The voices, combined with the tinkling of bells, beating of drums and gongs, and whirring of pigeon wings, made a kind of pleasant thrum, as if the country's big, pulsing heart rested just beneath this very patch of earth upon which he sat.

At last, he couldn't contain his curiosity, and he poked his head out from around the stone to look around. Just to peek. He didn't think anyone could see him.

The morning unfolded below him as the village awoke and

came to life. The women in their pretty nightgown-like dresses greeted one another as they passed. Saffron-robed monks floated up the steps to what Jack knew must be a temple. A man standing at a small shrine rang a bell, then clapped his hands and appeared to pray.

It was as different a scene as any he had ever observed, and yet something about it was so familiar: the way a mother smoothed her daughter's hair, a little boy chasing a butterfly. The way an old man stopped to stretch his back, or a dog plopping down and madly scratching his ear—these things were as familiar as the lark's song in the farmer's field.

And now, here was Yoshi, back again, giving him a scolding look, then gesturing for him to follow. And once again they climbed the hill into the forest, where they stopped by a clear, rushing brook.

The first thing to deal with was the smell, Yoshi decided. There was a peculiar barbarian smell that they would have to eliminate. A bath was needed, even if it was going to be in a cold stream instead of a hot spring. Yoshi pointed to the stream, and Jack seemed to understand. He climbed out of his clothes and into the chilly water.

The bath helped, Yoshi decided, and so did getting rid of the jacket and trousers, which were made of some thick, soft, but slightly scratchy fabric. The jacket might be warm in cool weather, but it smelled like a wet dog, and it had to go.

Now for the hair. Yoshi pushed Jack's head underwater. Jack came up, mad as a hissing otter, sputtering something that sounded like it might be a curse. When Yoshi pantomimed scrubbing his head, Jack scowled, but did as indicated and went under again, this time of his own accord.

Now, Yoshi thought, the barbarian was as ready as he'd ever be to climb into the clothing he had procured. Yes, it was an old woman's kimono, but Jack probably wouldn't know that, and it would be a good disguise. And the wide-brimmed wicker hat would keep his face covered.

Once Jack was dressed, Yoshi pursed his lips and frowned. Something was still wrong. Well, there were a lot of things wrong. The foreign boy didn't stand right or walk right. His arms were too long, and his legs too skinny, and too . . . white. That was it. Parts of him were entirely too white. His hands and face were browned from the sun, but his bare legs and arms where they showed were pale as frog bellies. *Well,* Yoshi thought, bending down to scoop up a handful of mud from the stream bank, *that can be remedied.*

Slap! On went the mud, onto Jack's bare legs. *I am touching a barbarian's skin,* Yoshi thought with a shudder. *Under this thin layer of mud slime is a barbarian's skin, and under the skin there's muscle and bone, and somewhere inside there beats a barbarian's heart, if they have them.* He wasn't sure. *Does a barbarian feel with his heart the things that I feel?* he wondered. *Does a barbarian feel anything the way I do?* He pinched Jack's skin.

Jack yelped and flicked some mud at Yoshi, freckling his face with muck. Jack guffawed at the sight. Yoshi scooped up a handful of mud and flung it. *Splat!* Wet muck hit Jack on the side of his face. Now it was Yoshi's turn to laugh. Soon mud was flying everywhere.

By the time they quit, they both were covered in mud, head to toe, and snorting with laughter.

After they had cleaned off their clothes and washed the mud from their skin and Jack had carefully reapplied the muck in the right places, they sat down and ate the bits of food Yoshi had brought: cubes of fried tofu, rice cakes, and a couple of pickled plums.

When they finished their meal, Yoshi gathered up Jack's clothes. He couldn't help but remember how he had traded clothes with Hideki. What would it be like to wear the clothes of *this* boy? he wondered. These narrow trousers? This smelly jacket? These strange shoes made out of the smooth skins of animals? He shivered a little when he touched them, and then he wrapped them, along with the jacket and trousers, in a square of colored cloth. This would keep the foreigner's clothes out of sight. He doubted that keeping the *foreigner* out of sight would be as easy.

35

FEET

Feet, feet, feet. That's all Jack could see with his head hidden under the wide-brimmed straw hat. Every time he tried to take a look around, Yoshi would whack him on the back, signaling that he must bow—Jack felt like he did nothing *but* bow! Mr. Obsqueakiness, he should be called. And so, instead of the wonders of a place unseen by any American before, all he saw were feet: dirty feet, clean feet, wide feet, skinny feet, chicken feet. He saw wooden sandals perched on blocks of wood. Straw sandals like the ones he was wearing. Dainty slippers. He saw the graceful hems of silk kimonos, the ragged edges of hemp trousers, bare legs and bare feet.

Most people couldn't see his face, but small children could. Some stared up at him, wide-eyed. Some cried and ran away. Others buried their faces in their mothers' skirts.

But even with his head down, staring at dirt roads and feet shuffling by, he could tell by the shadows and the sunlight that he and Yoshi were going north—away from the ships. Why?

After a time, it became apparent that they were coming to a city, a big city. Maybe, Jack thought, it was the famed

Edo street scene. (*Ando Hiroshige*)

forbidden city of Edo. The din, the bustle, the energy—he could hear and feel that. Voices called out, like the hawkers back home shouting out their wares. He heard the clatter of wooden clogs on the cobblestones, the clopping of horses' hooves, and, somewhere, the tolling of a deep-toned bell. If he tilted his head just a little, he could sometimes glimpse stands piled high with brightly colored fruits and vegetables: purple eggplants, dark leafy things or pale green stalks, giant white radishes, red-orange persimmons, and those beautiful oranges that were so sweet.

Aromas assailed him: steaming vegetables, grilling fish, smoky incense, the smoke of charcoal braziers and cooking fires, and always the briny smell of the sea, sharp and strong as seaweed.

Jack realized that Yoshi wanted him to keep his head down all the time, but he wasn't going to be the first American to enter Edo and not look! He peeked as much as he dared, trying not to let anyone see him, but he couldn't help but stare: Fishermen on stilts. Men wearing hardly a stitch of clothing carrying bundles or baskets of bamboo, or lumber, or fish. Women with babies on their backs. A barber shaving the sides of a man's head. A blacksmith heating iron in a red-hot forge. Two men in an open-air café, their chopsticks poised above their bowls. A man pushing a cart piled high with brooms and umbrellas and tools of all sorts.

He tried to capture in his memory little scenes that he could take home with him. But he couldn't keep from wondering, What if he never got home?

Still, he couldn't resist looking, at doorways hung with wares to sell—painted lanterns, baskets, silk and velvet garments, lacquered cups and bowls, and bamboo cages of all sizes: tiny ones holding singing crickets, and bigger ones containing birds. And then something Jack saw made him stop short: two large bamboo cages, each one holding a man.

"What are those—" he began, but Yoshi hushed him and hustled him away, though not before noticing that several people looked up or glanced their way, curious about the strange-sounding words.

Jack twisted around to look at Yoshi, but Yoshi hissed so ferociously at him that he ducked his head and shuffled along in the now familiar crouch.

When they finally were alone, Jack whispered to Yoshi, "Those men in those cages . . ."

Yoshi knew what Jack wanted to know. He tried to find the words to explain while also trying to make sense of it himself. He had recognized the men at once, and hoped they hadn't recognized him. Those two bushi were the ones who had wanted to go to America. And they had tried to go through with it. Yoshi had heard that much from the gossipers around the cages. They had gone to the ships, been rejected, been arrested by the authorities, and were being transported to an Edo prison.

Yoshi did not want to think what might happen to *him* if he were discovered taking an American to Edo.

Yoshi found that he was constantly thumping Jack on the back: one thump for not too low, two times to bow a little lower, and a hard press for "Deep bow! Deep bow!" Even so, Jack was fairly terrible at it, and Yoshi had to add a little apologetic nod of his head every time, as if to say, "I'm sorry, but my old grandmother is not quite right in the head. Please forgive her."

They had skirted the Kawasaki post station and managed to weave their way unheeded through Shinagawa station and crossed the Nihon Bridge without challenge by positioning themselves on the other side of a bunch of pack horses.

At the first moat, Yoshi got Jack through the gate simply by joking with the guards. "My old grandmother," he explained, while pressing firmly on Jack's back to keep him in a constant bowing position. "She has never been to Edo before and is overwhelmed."

The guards laughed and waved them through.

It was dark by the time they reached the stables, and that made it easier to sneak Jack and himself into Haru's stall. Yoshi checked on a leg wound she'd gotten a few days earlier, changing the bandage while Jack gathered up straw for their beds. Then, with a couple of straw piles for beds and more straw for coverlets, they tumbled, exhausted, into slumber.

In the morning, Yoshi went out to look for Manjiro.

He didn't have to look far. Manjiro was standing in the midst of a crowd of boys outside the stable doors.

"That's much better, Shozo," he was saying. "But make nice, long, lazy circles like this." Manjiro spun the lasso over his head and let go. The loop dropped over Yoshi. "Look what I caught!" Manjiro said.

The stableboys whooped with laughter.

Little Han ran to Yoshi and helped remove the loop from around his middle. "Where have you been?" Han said. "Your master's been looking for you."

Manjiro handed the coiled rope to Hiko and said, "Keep practicing! You're all showing improvement."

He took Yoshi by the arm and, saying, "We have work to do," began leading him away. Yoshi couldn't help but glance over his shoulder at the boys, who were all busy practicing with lassos. What had happened, he wondered, the short while he'd been away?

36

THE GIFTS

That's where the gifts are kept," Manjiro said, pointing to a large storehouse ahead of them.

"Gifts?" Yoshi said.

"Yes, from the Americans to the emperor and empress, the shogun, his commissioners. Actually, I don't think the Americans realize there is any difference between the shogun and the emperor. Because all the major gifts are addressed to the emperor and empress, and none to the shogun."

"If the shogun had allowed you to speak with the Americans, they would not have made such an embarrassing mistake," Yoshi said.

Manjiro chuckled. "They can't be embarrassed if they don't know they made a mistake, can they?" he said. "And, anyway, perhaps the Japanese gift givers should be embarrassed themselves. I have heard of the gifts given to the Americans, and I fear they will think the gifts cheap, and not understand their symbolic meaning."

"What do you mean?" Yoshi asked.

"The Americans probably wonder why the value of the

gifts does not seem high, without realizing that, for us, a high material value would seem like a bribe, which would be an insult to an honorable recipient," Manjiro explained. "Instead, we give gifts with symbolic meaning. But they wouldn't understand that, either. Here we take for granted that everyone understands the symbolism of the gifts we give. A fan, because of the way it gets wider, or 'wealthier,' toward its end, is a way of saying, 'We wish you greater and greater wealth.' It is a way of wishing the recipient prosperity. *You* know that, and *I* know that, but Americans do *not* know that. They don't have the same customs we do."

Yoshi nodded. He hadn't really thought about it. Now would be a good time to bring up the American boy, he supposed. He glanced around and noticed the two officials who had been trailing them—no doubt the shogun's spies. At the moment they stood far enough away that he could maybe whisper something. But he hesitated, trying to find the right words, and Manjiro went on, "Did anyone from the Japanese delegation seek to explain any of this to the Americans? Probably not. So the Americans go away thinking they have been given nothing of value. Which in their minds is an insult."

"It is a mistake that they didn't send you, sir," Yoshi said, bowing to Manjiro, "for there is no one who understands their minds as you do." *Now*, he thought, *now I must say something about Jack,* but they had come to the door, where two unfriendly looking guards were stationed.

Yoshi could see that talking about Jack was going to have to wait.

After Manjiro showed them some official-looking papers, the guards opened the door and gestured for them to enter. Yoshi couldn't help but notice that both the trailing officials *and* the guards also followed them inside.

"It is my job to catalog and explain all these things," Manjiro said.

Yoshi stared in wonder at the many and unusual items. The Americans had not spared any expense, that was clear. There were boats, carts, wagons, many kinds of tools, and something called a telegraph machine that could send messages in a kind of magical way. Most wondrous of all, a working railroad, smaller in size than a real one, Manjiro said, with several train cars, each big enough to hold a person or two.

Yoshi wandered around, looking at all the things while keeping an eye on the lurking officials and the two hovering guards. Meanwhile, Manjiro took notes. So many things, American things. What was it about them that made them so distinctly foreign? What *was* it? Was it that they were just so . . . functional, without regard to beauty or form?

In his country, no matter how ordinary or trivial a thing—an iron kettle, a paper lantern, a bamboo curtain, a wooden pillow—it was made by hand and crafted to be a thing of beauty.

The gifts from the Americans were cold, strong, practical things meant for plowing earth or harvesting grains.

Manjiro went about pointing at and naming them, often using the English word for the item. "These are meant for the emperor," he said. "*Maps* of states and *lithographs*, *telescope* and stand, *sheet-iron stove*, *rifles*, *muskets*, *swords*."

"*Swords*," Yoshi repeated.

"*Pistols*," Manjiro continued. "A silver-topped *dressing case*, yards of broadcloth and *velvet*. A pocket *watch*." Manjiro said "watch" in English, adding that it was one of those American words that meant more than one thing. "It refers to a timepiece, but can also mean *watch* with your eyes."

"*Watch*," Yoshi repeated. How could he ask to learn the English words that would be useful in order to talk to Jack? Things like "Stay here," "Don't move," "I'll come back." And "How do you plan to get back to your ship? Any ideas? Keep your head down, you idiot! Don't you have any manners in your country? Are you hungry? Thirsty? Tired?" But he couldn't ask. The guards were always nearby.

"*Champagne, tea, casks of whiskey, bottles of cordial*, and *cases of champagne*," Manjiro rattled on in English. "*Clocks, stoves, perfumes, farm tools*, and *seeds*." The words were as strange as the items. "*Boat*," he said, pointing to a copper-sided boat.

"*Boat*," Yoshi repeated. That would be a handy word to know. It would be an even handier thing to have.

One couldn't help but be impressed by the cleverness of some of the gifts, or at least the unusualness. But nothing struck Yoshi as really *beautiful* until he laid eyes on the books. Nine large volumes, filled with paintings of birds. Here was something truly elegant, fit for the emperor. In fact, Manjiro said, "These are meant for the emperor." He added under his breath that he doubted the shogun intended to send them to him.

"May I look?" Yoshi said.

Manjiro glanced at the guards, then opened a book. "*Birds of America*," he said. "By an artist named Audubon."

There were birds of scarlet, orange, and blue, and one long-necked bird of the deepest pink. Some birds Yoshi knew, and some he had never before seen. The birds perched on branches thick with blossoms or berries, hid in thickets, or floated on glassy ponds. The images were elegant, colorful, detailed.

That the barbarians could make iron tools, guns, and other weapons did not surprise Yoshi. But no "offal-eating demon" could have made these pictures, he thought as he turned the pages. What especially caught and held his attention were the backgrounds, the landscapes of these faraway places. Swamps, misty hills, rocky coasts, and stormy seas.

On one page, a teal-colored heron stood in a river on whose far-off sunlit banks stood tall, tufted trees. The river disappeared around a bend that Yoshi found himself staring at, as if he might—if he looked hard enough—see around it, see what lay around that bend.

For a moment, looking at these pictures, he could almost forget about the boy back at the stables, hidden in the straw.

"Louisiana Heron" from *Birds of America* by John James Audubon.

He was almost—just for a few glorious moments—transported to a glistening river, into tall grasses, on the shores of an ocean far, far away.

"*Louisiana heron.*" The voice in Yoshi's ear startled him.

"What?" Yoshi said.

"That is the name of that bird," Manjiro said. "It lives in a place called *Louisiana*, in the United States."

"How did you learn to read the language of the outsiders?"

"English, you mean?" Manjiro asked. "I went to school in America. I learned many things: English, mathematics, and, especially interesting to me, navigation. This is something the Westerners understand much more fully than we do. And it is why they can sail all over this vast earth."

Yoshi's eyes drifted back to the picture of the heron and the mesmerizing blue-green world in which it lived.

"Perhaps one day you will sail to that place, *Louisiana*," Manjiro said, "and see it for yourself."

Yoshi shook his head. Such a thing was unimaginable. But he couldn't help thinking of Kiku, and how she wanted to go to the wooded hills and mountains beyond the shogun's garden. He imagined telling her about these pictures, and how he had felt that same desire—to go beyond what you could see. It was just a nameless longing, really, to see more, to know more, maybe even to *be* more.

He took one final look at the picture, trying to remember it exactly so he could describe it to Kiku, and then Manjiro closed the book.

"There is much we can learn from the Westerners," Manjiro said. "I hope our countrymen will welcome them and accept them here."

"There are those who say they will destroy our way of life," Yoshi said.

"Well," Manjiro replied, "we shall see. Some things it would be good to change. Some things will have to change. And some things may change that we wish would not. But that is the way of life, is it not?"

Maybe, Yoshi thought, everything could remain the same except a few Americans would show up to trade at a couple of remote ports far from Edo. Probably, Yoshi thought, life would just go on as normal.

But when he gazed around at the things the Americans had sent, he knew it would not. People would want these things. They would want other things the Americans brought. He himself would like some of those fire sticks that Jack had.

People would want the knowledge of the Americans, as Manjiro said. But some people would not want any of the changes; some of them would be willing to fight to prevent it. And what would happen then?

Now, Yoshi thought, as he followed Manjiro out of the storehouse, *tell him about Jack*. He stepped closer to Manjiro and opened his mouth to speak, but heard the guard behind him whisper, "That man"— Yoshi glanced back to see the guard following Manjiro with his eyes. "There is an extra watch on him, now that the barbarians have returned."

The other guard agreed. "He is not to be trusted. The councillors say that he should be 'treated generously while guarded closely.'"

What had he been thinking? Yoshi wondered. Of course he couldn't involve Manjiro in his troubles! If Manjiro were to be discovered associating in any way with an American, it would prove that he was a spy. It would be just what his enemies wanted.

No, he was going to have to figure out what to do with Jack on his own. And that meant that he needed to get back to the stables right away!

But just then, out of the corner of his eye, he caught the flapping of sleeves and the fluttering of fans, the scurrying and whispering of messages being passed. Suddenly messengers were among them, saying, "The shogun's advisers wish to speak with you." And, just like that, Manjiro and Yoshi were whisked away.

As they were escorted across the moat to the gate, Yoshi

felt chilled to his core. *They've discovered Jack,* he thought. *And now we three will be punished: Jack and I, and Manjiro, too. It's my fault for leaving Jack for so long. I should never have left him. It was stupid to bring him to Edo.*

He felt his heart sinking lower and lower as they wended their way farther and farther into the interior of the castle.

37

BASEBALL

You're up next," Jack told the little kid, handing him the bamboo stick.

Three other stableboys were positioned at rough approximations of first, second, and third base. Jack had made the biggest boy the pitcher. Then, in order to show them how it was done, he had been the first up to bat himself.

The big kid had thrown Jack a perfect pitch, and Jack hit "the ball"—a wadded-up bunch of cloth bandages—out of the park. Well, not really, but it landed in some kind of canal, and while the boys ran over to fish it out, Jack ran the bases, cheering for himself as he slid into home.

The boys caught on fast, and soon they were arguing over the rules. At least that's what it sounded like to Jack. He laughed. They sounded like his friends back home—different language, same arguments.

While they argued, he leaned on the "bat" and took a look around. These were some impressive stables, he thought. Whoever owned these buildings and these small but sturdy-looking horses must be a rich so-and-so.

He'd been awakened by one of those horses earlier that morning when its tail kept switching him in the face. He'd opened his eyes to see a horse's rear end and nobody else— Yoshi was gone.

But he had caught a glimpse of something between the slats in the stall door. Eyes. Many eyes staring at him through the cracks. Then heads: nine heads appeared over the top of the door, staring down at him.

Just kids. Still, he'd thought, better safe than sorry. He groped around in the straw for something with which to protect himself, and his hand came upon a length of bamboo, buried under the straw. He grabbed the stick and, not wanting to be cornered in the stall, unlatched the door and stepped out.

A lot of curious horses and a gang of kids—stableboys, he reckoned—that's all there was. He stood with crossed arms and glowered at them while they stared back at him. This time he was going to take a stand: absolutely no bowing to these ragamuffins!

There was some giggling, and by their whispering and gesturing, he got the distinct impression that he had been dressed up as a girl. How could anyone ever tell? It seemed to him that everybody, male and female, dressed in the same silk petticoats.

One of the boys, the tallest and apparently also the bravest, crept toward Jack and touched his hair, then pretended to be burned, which made the others laugh. Jack rolled his eyes. This was the oldest joke in the book. If he'd had a half dime every time a kid back home tried that trick, he'd be as wealthy as John Jacob Astor.

Now the others were creeping closer, also wanting to touch his red hair, he supposed, but he'd put a stop to that.

He tossed a stone up in the air, hit it with the stick, and asked, "You fellows know how to play baseball?"

The boys settled their argument, and next up was the littlest kid. Jack showed him how to stand and how to swing the bat when the "ball" came over the plate. The kid smacked it and made a run for third base, but Jack nabbed him and sent him in the other direction. The outfielder fumbled the ball, and the boy circled the bases, stomping triumphantly on the dusty old straw mat that was home plate.

"You're a natural!" Jack said, patting him on the back.

"Natcha!" the kid shouted.

Then Jack was up to bat again. He kicked his long "petticoat" behind him, tapped the bat against the plate, and, when the ball came at him, bunted. He dropped the bat and charged for first base, but his foot caught in his skirt, and down he went, into the dust. The boys howled with laughter.

A shadow seemed to pass over the sun, the boys' laughter stopped abruptly, and Jack felt a big hand close around his arm.

38

IN THE SHOGUN'S CASTLE

The courtyard garden outside the reception room was a profusion of cherry blossoms. This did nothing to lift Yoshi's mood as he knelt outside the room, waiting for the meeting to begin.

He heard the rustle of silk and brocades and the murmur of voices as the councillors arrived and arranged themselves inside the room. Then one cleared his throat and Yoshi squeezed his eyes shut, waiting for the blow.

"What does it mean that at this very moment the Black Ships are approaching Edo?" the councillor asked Manjiro. "Will the barbarians dare to enter our sacred city?"

Yoshi's eyes flew open. The ships were coming to Edo?

"Do the barbarians intend to invade?" one of the councillors asked, adding that they had been told in the strictest terms not to approach the city.

Yoshi breathed a sigh of relief. So this wasn't about Jack. He hadn't been discovered hiding in the stables. Not yet, anyway.

The councillors continued their questions, wanting to know what the barbarians intended to do next.

Manjiro answered calmly that he didn't know, he didn't fully understand their motivations, but he would assume that the American commodore was simply curious and wanted a closer look at the famous city of Edo. Westerners were naturally curious, Manjiro told them. "That is why their learning is constantly becoming greater and greater."

"This breach of the edict cannot be tolerated!" a councillor insisted.

"We have already suffered humiliation at the hands of the barbarians. This is too much!" asserted another.

In the garden, Yoshi noticed a familiar figure clipping dead twigs from a cherry tree. Kiku. He thought of how he wanted to tell her about the pictures of the birds and describe the bend in the river and how he had wanted to go there to see what lay beyond that bend, in just the same way she wanted to go to the faraway mountain beyond the shogun's garden.

"Kiku," he whispered.

She turned just as Yoshi heard a councillor's voice say, "There are rumors that there is an American in Edo."

Yoshi froze.

"A barbarian spy within our midst!" the councillor finished.

Yoshi's heart hammered in his ears so loudly that he didn't hear anything else. Did they know about Jack after all? He had to get back to the stables as fast as he could. But how? How would he find his way through the palace's serpentine corridors, or get past the dozens of checkpoints, gates, and hundreds of armed guards and sentries? Without Manjiro, he wouldn't be able to go anywhere!

Kiku looked at Yoshi from under her gardener's hat. Her arched eyebrow and flashing eyes wordlessly asked, "Do you know something about this?"

He thought of how she seemed to appear and disappear so easily. How did she do that? And where did she go? Did he dare ask her to help him? He had to risk it.

"I have to get back to the stables right away," he whispered. "Can you help me?"

A smile flickered across Kiku's face. "Follow me. But make sure you keep up." She disappeared behind the shrubs.

Yoshi followed her, but once again, when he stepped behind the greenery, all he saw was the long, impenetrable hedge. Kiku was nowhere to be seen!

Then a tiny motion like a bird flitting into the hedge caught his eye, and when he looked he saw it was not a bird at all, but a small foot disappearing into the foliage!

Yoshi raced to the spot to see that a wooden tub—a tub with no bottom—had been shoved into the hedge, and it was through this that Kiku had disappeared. He bent down and saw her hand, gesturing to him to crawl through.

After he wiggled through, Kiku pulled out the tub, and the branches sprang back into place, as if nothing at all had just happened there.

The two of them dashed past a group of startled washerwomen who sat ripping the stitches out of kimonos, then past another group washing the long pieces of cloth, and finally past those who were hanging the wet fabric to dry. The women looked up in surprise as Kiku and Yoshi raced past.

Into the washhouse and out, through the back doors of servants' quarters, and along alleyways they went. Yoshi panted out an explanation to Kiku as they climbed through hedges, under fences, up and over walls, employing ropes, buckets, and all manner of things that Kiku seemed to find, quite remarkably, hidden under shrubs or steps or behind doors.

Yoshi started to think about what he might say to Kiku when they reached the stables. He would thank her, but what could he say so that he might be sure to see her again?

Then suddenly he was standing in the wide, gravel exercise yard of the stables. He turned to thank Kiku, but she had already disappeared back into the labyrinth of the castle buildings.

At the stables, Yoshi confronted the row of sheepish-looking boys. "Where is he?" he asked them. "What did you do with him?" Glancing around, he noticed a bamboo stick lying in the dirt.

"We didn't do nothing!" Han squeaked.

"Where *is* he?" Yoshi demanded again, still staring at the length of bamboo. He recognized it. It was his practice katana. Lying there in the dirt, though, it looked like nothing special— just an ordinary stick.

"Hiko?" Yoshi turned his eyes on the leader of the boys.

Hiko cleared his throat. "Bushi . . ."

Yoshi felt a flutter of fear. "How many?" he asked.

Hiko held up one finger.

"Just one? One? And you let him take Jack? Why didn't you stop him?" Yoshi asked.

The boys stared at Yoshi, mouths agape. Yoshi knew what they were thinking: Who would ever go against even one samurai?

"What did he look like, this bushi?" Yoshi asked.

"He was big," Han said.

"He walked like this." Enju stamped his feet.

"He had a long blue scar on his face," Hiko said. "And he was looking for you."

Yoshi steeled himself. Now, instead of running away from Kitsune, Yoshi would have to go looking for him.

PART FIVE
AIR

When your spirit is not in the least clouded, when the
cloud of bewilderment is cleared away, there is the Void.

—Miyamoto Musashi, *The Book of Five Rings*

39

THE ASSIGNMENT

Yoshi was pretty sure he knew where he would find Kitsune. The big bushi and the others would be sitting in the soba shop arguing about what to do with the barbarian boy. Someone would suggest that they should keep the boy as a hostage and make demands, but Kitsune would advocate for slicing his head off and putting it on a pole as a warning to other barbarians.

As Yoshi hurried away from the stables, crossed the outer moat, and worked his way through the streets, he considered his situation. There would be several samurai. They would be armed. He doubted he could march in there and just demand that they release the boy.

For one thing, Kitsune was sure to want Yoshi's head as well.

Maybe he could challenge Kitsune to a fight. Maybe someone would lend him a katana. He'd lose, of course. But maybe not. Kitsune was strong and big and he had a lot of power in his sword arm, but he was also reckless and undisciplined. There might be an opportunity . . .

As soon as he rounded the last corner, he saw Needs-a-Shave leaning against the doorframe of the soba shop. He still needed a shave. Yoshi ducked behind a wall and waited until he went in. Then Yoshi took a deep breath, made himself as tall as he could, smoothed his peasant's clothes, and walked inside.

The bushi were huddled at a low table in a shadowy corner. Jack was sitting on a chair—a small courtesy for the foreigner—with his hands tied behind his back. He gave Yoshi an apologetic smile. Yoshi was surprised how glad he was to see him, but he didn't smile back.

The others looked up from their cups of tea. Kuma glowered. The tall, lean one was occupied with a fit of coughing. Catfish pulled on his whiskers. Loose-Hair was nowhere to be seen. In one corner, a cook sat chopping vegetables at a low table.

And, standing in the shadowy fringes, Kitsune.

"I suppose you've come to retrieve your little friend," Kitsune said. He stepped forward and nodded toward Jack. That's when Yoshi noticed a big purple bruise spreading around one of Kitsune's eyes. Yoshi's eyes flicked toward Jack, who smirked. Jack had given him that black eye! The growing bruise didn't obscure the poisonous hatred in the big bushi's eyes.

"You know it's a mistake to keep him here," Yoshi said. "If the authorities find out you've been holding him, you will be in big trouble. They know about him; they're looking for him. The Black Ships are on their way here now. You realize that an incident such as this could start a full-scale war!"

The others shifted their weight nervously. Maybe, Yoshi thought, maybe he would be able to talk them into releasing Jack. "And if the Americans find out you are keeping him prisoner, I shudder to think what will happen to you!"

The lean one bit his lip. Kuma blinked rapidly. Only Kitsune kept his narrowed eyes focused on Yoshi. "The Black Ships have turned around," he said. "They are going away."

Was Kitsune bluffing? Or did he know something Jack didn't know?

"Yes," Coughing One agreed. "It is true. The ships are going away. They have headed back to Kanagawa."

Chop chop chop went the cook's knife.

"Even so," Kitsune said, "war is exactly what we need. If not now, when? If we wait, we will be crushed. The spirit of our divine land will, like a light, be extinguished!"

"A little over-dramatic, wouldn't you say?" Needs-a-Shave commented.

"We must send a message to the shogun that barbarians will not be tolerated in our land," Kitsune went on. "Here is this one"—he gestured toward Jack—"spying! In the sacred city of Edo! He deserves to die."

Yoshi glanced around. The others looked pensive. "Let him go," Needs-a-Shave said. "You know that it's trouble to have him here. Now is not the time to start a conflict. We must be better prepared to truly fight the outsiders."

"I say we put his head on a pole," Kitsune said. "An example of what happens to barbarians who trespass on sacred ground!"

"Do you think the Americans won't sneeze?" said Coughing One. "Indeed they will! A sneeze with a blast of gunpowder weighted with cannonballs!"

Chop chop chop went the cook's knife.

Yoshi watched Jack's eyes flit from one speaker to another. He was glad Jack couldn't understand exactly what they said, even though he must have a pretty good idea what they were talking about.

"He's just a boy," said Needs-a-Shave. "You should set him loose. What harm can he do?"

"I wouldn't be so sure about that," said Kuma. "He's as wily as a fox. And look at his eyes."

They all peered at Jack's eyes, wincing a bit at the strange blueness of them.

"What about them?"

"Even though he's a barbarian, he is not without intelligence,"

Kuma said. "You can see that he's thinking. I don't know about what, but about something."

Jack was thinking that the knot these desperadoes had tied around his wrists was a good one, and now that he had managed to loosen his hands a bit, he could feel it with his fingertips. Being a sailor, he figured he knew just about every knot there was, but he didn't know this one.

The cook, who had been chopping onions, got up, sniffed, and wiped his sleeve across his eyes. *You might well weep*, Jack thought. The cook picked up the bowl of onions and carried them into the kitchen, leaving the knife lying on the table. Jack averted his eyes from it, shifting them back on the group of samurai, all of whom had been staring at him. But as soon as he turned his gaze on them, they looked away.

"It's too dangerous to kill him," Catfish said. "They won't let a slight like that go unpunished, even if he is only a worthless spy. Even if it were only one of their *dogs*, they would take revenge."

"Better than killing the little barbarian would be to make an example of the outsider spy, Nakahama. As we intended to do in the first place," said Kuma. "At least that would not start a war with the Americans. He is not, after all, one of them."

"Nor is he one of us," sneered Kitsune. "I see the sense in what you say." He turned his evil eye on Yoshi. "Perhaps this little peasant is just the person we need. Perhaps he can do the job for us."

Yoshi did not want to think what the "job" was.

"Here's a commoner who thinks he knows how to use a katana." Kitsune unconsciously touched his scar, while the other men's eyes darted from Kitsune to Yoshi to one another.

Yoshi tried to keep his face an impassive mask, while wondering what Kitsune was getting at.

"But he is just a boy!" Needs-a-Shave said. "You can't—"

Kitsune cut him off. "Yes, he is just a boy. So no one will suspect him. As a trusted servant, he can get himself into the compound. He seems to think he knows how to use a sword. Let's find out if he really can. Let *him* get rid of the American spy."

"Wait a minute . . . ," Yoshi said. "You're not suggesting— you're not saying that I . . . ?" His mouth went dry. He felt like a completely empty shell, a husk. A puff of wind could have carried him away.

Kitsune smiled, and it was not a pretty sight. The scar on his cheek pulled his lip in a funny direction, so it was hard to tell if he was smiling or sneering. "Do you want the little barbarian to survive?" He nodded toward Jack. "Or your friend the spy? It's going to be one or the other. Which one do you choose?"

40

A WASP STINGING
A WEEPING FACE

hich will it be?" Kitsune asked again. "We will release the boy if you dispatch Manjiro."

"Dispatch?"

Kitsune drew a finger across his neck. "Or," he said, "we will dispatch this one," he nodded at Jack, "and leave Manjiro alone. So which will it be?"

Yoshi swallowed and said, "Nakahama." He couldn't bring himself to say the name by which he had always called his friend, Manjiro.

Kitsune leveled his gaze at Yoshi. "You must bring us some proof that he is dead."

"Bring us his head," Kuma growled.

Yoshi felt as if he were going to vomit.

"He can't be expected to get out of the compound and all the way here carrying a bloody, dripping head," Needs-a-Shave said.

"That's true," Coughing One agreed. "What he says is true."

"I'll bring you," Yoshi said, picturing Manjiro's unused daisho, "his katana."

"With his blood on it," Kitsune demanded.

His blood! Yoshi flinched.

"Well?" Kuma said when Yoshi did not immediately respond.

"Of course his blood will be on it!" Yoshi cried. "Who else's blood would it be?"

"And Kuma here will go with you," Kitsune said.

"That won't work!" Yoshi blurted out.

"Oh?" Kitsune said.

"I mean . . ." Yoshi hesitated. "I can pass by the guards, but how will he?"

"Well, you'll just have to figure some other way for you both, won't you? Do you think we're just going to let you go alone?"

Yoshi didn't respond.

"Well, then." Kitsune narrowed his eyes to such a narrow slit that nothing could be seen of them but a thin black gleam. "Return with the outsider's blade at the hour of the rat."

Now Yoshi and Kuma walked alongside each other through the dark streets toward the Egawa compound, where Manjiro was staying. Kuma shifted the lantern in his hand and grunted. "Have you come up with a plan?" he asked.

They were almost at Lord Egawa's mansion, and Yoshi still didn't know what to do! He had chosen Manjiro only because that choice would give him more time to think. But he hadn't come up with anything. All he could think of was the proverb "A wasp stinging a weeping face." That's what his life was like right now—insult heaped upon injury.

He had to stop feeling sorry for himself and come up with something!

Well, he had *one* idea, and he reminded himself of Miyamoto Musashi's words: "Even a road of one thousand miles can only be traversed by taking one step at a time." Or one *idea* at a time. That's what he had: exactly *one* idea.

He veered onto a route that brought them to the stables. "I need to get something," he told Kuma. "You wait here."

"No," Kuma said. "I go with you."

"Fine," Yoshi said. "But be quiet."

Kuma nodded and the two stole inside the dark stable.

The horses were all in their stalls quietly munching hay or resting. Near Haru's stall, Yoshi found an old wooden feed tub. He kicked the bottom out of it.

"Is this part of your plan?" Kuma asked.

Haru looked up and whinnied.

"Shh," Yoshi said. "You'll rile the horses."

Yoshi checked Haru's bandaged leg, then touched her nose before going out. "See you later, my friend," he said, adding, "if all goes well."

Kuma followed Yoshi as he crept around the back of the stables, then along the hedge to a spot where Yoshi stopped, glanced around to make sure no one was looking, and crammed the bottomless tub into the thick tangle of branches. Then, sucking his breath in and trying to be as skinny as possible, he wriggled through it, just the way he and Kiku had done earlier. He was maybe not as graceful as Kiku, and he had to kick and push and struggle a bit. But he soon found himself on the other side, crouched behind the rhododendrons in the Egawa garden.

He turned around, stuck his head into the barrel, and said to Kuma, "Now you."

"I can't get through that thing!" Kuma said.

"Hmm," Yoshi replied. "I suppose you're right. Wait there, then, and I'll be back soon."

"No!" Kuma's voice was a harsh whisper. "I'm supposed to go with you!"

"It's the only way in!" Yoshi said. "It's not my fault you're too big to get through. But don't worry, I won't tell anyone that you didn't come inside the compound. Anyway, this way you don't run the risk of being caught by the guards."

Kuma was silent, probably pondering that bit of good luck, and Yoshi hurried away.

◆ ◆ ◆

Where was the katana? Yoshi wondered. It must be resting on the rack for that purpose in the entryway of Manjiro's chambers.

Yoshi crept around the garden pond and tiptoed over a little wooden bridge, then stepped out of his sandals and silently slid his bare feet along the wooden walkway that led along the courtyard.

Here is where the floor squeaked, he remembered. Skirting the noisy spot, he continued on his way, the pale moon his only light.

It was a wonder, he thought, that the loud thumping of his heart didn't awaken the entire household! Past room after room . . . Finally he stood before Manjiro's door. There he stopped.

Slowly and quietly, he slid open the door, pushing a little each time Manjiro exhaled. When the door was opened just enough, he slipped inside.

Moonlight slipped into the room with him, casting its blue light along the tatami floor, over Manjiro's sleeping form, and illuminating the scabbards of the swords, placed on a special rack just inside the door. Yoshi crept to it and lifted the katana.

Slowly he drew the blade from its scabbard. Moonlight struck the steel, making it seem as transparent as air, as reflecting as water. For a moment, it was as if he held a slice of sky in his hands, or a ribbon of faraway ocean. But as he turned it slightly, the light struck the blade's sharp and deadly edge—its killing edge—and Yoshi felt as if the point had been thrust into his own heart.

Katana. (*Yuko Shimizu*)

41

THE COOK'S KNIFE

From across the room, Jack spied the knife blade glinting from under the vegetables.

After Yoshi had gone, the others left the room. They had tied a mean knot, Jack thought, but they didn't seem to completely understand chairs. For instance, they didn't seem to realize that just because you were tied to one didn't mean you couldn't move.

Jack and the chair hopped across the room, somewhat painfully, until he reached the table. There was the knife—right there! But how to get the knife into his hands? The table was so low!

In order to get to the knife, he would have to either tip the chair forward, fall on his face, and pick the knife up in his teeth or tip the chair backward. Since his hands were behind him, it made more sense to do the latter.

He hopped himself and the chair around, and prepared to do the thing for which his mother had often scolded him: rocking on the back legs of his chair. "One day you're going to tip over backward and crack your skull!" she'd barked, and now, he supposed, he was about to do exactly that.

He rocked on the back legs of the chair until the thing tipped all the way over—and landed splat in the middle of the vegetables, his head smashing into a pile of mushrooms. *Fortunately,* he thought, *mushrooms are soft as far as vegetables go.*

He groped about in the sorry mess until his fingers touched the cold, smooth, sharp blade. Jack smiled. It was just where he wanted it to be.

42

WINNING WITHOUT THE SWORD

Yoshi's heels tapped along the dark streets, while Kuma huffed and puffed behind him. Otherwise, the streets were silent now, at the cusp of the hours of the rat and the ox.

"I don't see why you had to stop at the stable," Kuma said. "That slowed us down."

"I told you," Yoshi said. "I had to return the feed tub."

"*Pffft*," Kuma scoffed. "An old bucket with the bottom missing! Who cares about that?"

Yoshi didn't answer. He was thinking through what had happened after he'd drawn the katana from its scabbard in Manjiro's room. For a moment, he indulged himself, appreciating the beauty of the blade, before feeling the crushing weight of his assignment. Then he'd heard a voice.

"What kind of trouble have you gotten yourself into," the familiar voice had said, "that you need a sword?"

Yoshi turned to see Manjiro watching him.

The two had conversed, Yoshi trying to explain how he had gotten himself into so much trouble, and now there was a plan of sorts. It had some rough edges, and he gnawed at something

Manjiro had told him. "Although you now have a katana," he'd said, "it will turn out better if you can 'win without the sword.'"

Yoshi could not imagine how that would be possible.

He and Kuma rounded the corner of the last street and turned into the alley, where four men waited in the shadows: Coughing One, Needs-a-Shave, Catfish, and Kitsune. Kitsune reached out for the bundle Yoshi carried, but Yoshi pointed to the restaurant. "I want to see the American first," he said.

They walked inside to where Jack was still sitting in the chair with his arms behind his back, just as they had left him.

"What a mess!" Catfish said, kicking at the vegetables strewn across the floor. "That cook is a slob."

"Let us see the blade," Kitsune said.

Yoshi unwrapped the bundle to reveal the katana. Even in the dim light, it was obvious that the blade was smeared with blood.

Catfish stuck his finger in it and said, "Still fresh."

"How do we know it's Nakahama's blood?" said Coughing One, taking the sword and examining it closely.

"Kuma can tell us." Kitsune stuck his chin out at the bear-like man. "He can say whose blood this is."

All eyes turned to Kuma.

Yoshi looked at him, too. Would he tell them that he had waited outside the compound while Yoshi had gone in alone?

Or that they'd stopped at the stables, where Kuma had again waited while Yoshi had gone inside? Had Kuma noticed that the blood didn't appear on the blade until after Yoshi had gone inside the mare's stall?

"Who else's would it be?" Kuma said, looking at no one.

Kitsune's eyes narrowed at Kuma, who shifted from one foot to the other, as if trying to find a relaxed way to stand. Then Kitsune turned his eyes on Yoshi. "So, perhaps you killed him, but perhaps you did not. We'll find out soon enough."

"Exactly so," Yoshi agreed. "Now I have fulfilled my part of the bargain, and you must fulfill yours. You must release the American."

"Just one final formality," Kitsune said. "I want you to put it in writing that you killed Manjiro."

"What for?"

"It will make the paperwork on my end so much easier."

"Paperwork?"

"Just do it, if you want the barbarian released."

Kitsune swept the remaining vegetables off the table and set down paper, brush, and ink bowl, then gestured for Yoshi to sit.

Yoshi picked up the brush and pressed it into the ink bowl. Out of the corner of his eye, he watched Coughing One slowly wiping the blood off the sword's blade.

"Have it say, 'I killed Nakahama Manjiro,'" Kitsune demanded.

Yoshi wrote it down.

"'On this day in the Month of New Life, seventh year of Kaei,'" Kitsune continued.

As he wrote, Yoshi thought, *Well, it is not going to make any difference what I write, because the man is alive, so clearly I couldn't have killed him.* He was pleased that his ruse had worked and that Kitsune had been so easily deceived.

But as he dipped the brush again, he began to wonder if this paperwork was for some other purpose. Maybe Kitsune wasn't as oafish as he thought. Maybe he *was* as sly as a fox. He would get Yoshi to confess in writing that he had killed Manjiro, and then Kitsune would be free to do it himself with impunity, since a confession had already been signed. Not only that, but Kitsune could kill Yoshi without any pesky questions, either, since he could tell the authorities he'd cut down a murderer.

But there was nothing Yoshi could do about it now. Kitsune had already plucked up the paper, blown on it to dry the ink, rolled it up, and shoved it inside his kimono.

Kitsune made a sound deep in his throat, then spoke: "Now, little samurai, it is time for you to earn your reward." Without hesitation, Kitsune drew his katana.

Yoshi snatched up the only thing at hand, the brush, as if to defend himself with it, which made Kitsune tip his head back and roar with laughter. When Kitsune's head tipped forward again, Yoshi flicked the brush at him, spraying ink into his eyes.

Kitsune clutched his face and roared again, this time in pain.

Yoshi dropped the brush and dashed toward Jack, but Coughing One stepped between them, brandishing Manjiro's clean and gleaming sword.

At that very moment, startling everyone, Jack stood up, lifted the chair he'd been sitting in over his head, and brought it down with a *cra-ack* on Coughing One's head. *So that's what that strange barbarian item is for,* Yoshi thought, as the man slumped to the ground. *It has a useful purpose after all.*

As Jack and Yoshi ran toward the door with the other three bushi in pursuit, Jack grabbed the ink bowl and whipped it at the closest one, hitting him squarely between the eyes. Yoshi snagged the dropped sword and scabbard.

The two boys bolted into the alley. For a moment, Jack thought they would escape, but then Yoshi tripped over a sack of rice and Jack slipped on something—sodden onion skins, it smelled like—and they both went down.

Say your prayers, Jack Sullivan, Jack thought as the desperadoes closed in on them. But a pattering sound above them diverted their attention to the roofs overhead.

All at once, the quiet was pierced with screeching and squealing, as if a flock of winged demons were arriving from the sky. The air was filled with silvery spinning loops of rope, and the alleyway became a blur—not of winged spirits but of boys. Boys leaping from the rooftops, lassos spinning.

"Well, I'll be . . . ," Jack said. He would not have guessed the lasso was in popular use in Japan.

Yoshi grabbed his arm and, once again, they ran.

During their flight, Jack tried to tuck little images into his memory: pools of lantern light on the damp streets, the glowing paper walls of houses and tea shops, a door sliding open, people staring up from their soup bowls as the boys rushed past, then out through another sliding paper door into a dark alley; women with white-painted faces and elaborate hairdos teetering on high wooden sandals; the reflections in the black canal water as they climbed into a boat, with a man standing in the back with a long pole.

There was only one other man in the boat. He smiled at the boys, and offered them dried persimmons and little balls made of sticky rice.

"Pleased to make your acquaintance," the man said to Jack.

Had that man just spoken in English, or was Jack losing his mind?

"Are you quite all right? No injuries?"

"You speak English . . . ," Jack began.

The man nodded. "You aren't hurt?" he repeated.

Jack shook his head. *The one man in all of Japan who can speak English*, Jack thought, *and I found him.*

As the boatman pushed the boat downriver, the man, whose name was Manjiro, told Jack how he had come to learn English, about his time in America, and some of the things he had learned there.

"With the new developments in transportation and communication, countries can no longer expect to live in isolation," he said. "But I believe that good will come out of this changing world."

The boat came out from under overhanging trees, and the dark sky spread out above them, dotted with bright stars.

"There is the Milky Way," Manjiro said, pointing to the thick streak of stars in the sky. "Here we call it the River of Heaven. It is said that it separates a pair of lovers—a farmhand and a princess. A sad story. But that same river of stars unites you and me, for we see the same stars when we look up from our very different places on earth. As a sailor, you know that those stars show us how to find each other."

Yoshi listened to the strange language for a while as the boat plied the Sumida River. Through the dark night they went, with the lingering scent of simmered broths and grilled fish still hanging in the air, and the fragrance of flowering shrubs and trees exploding in little bursts.

It was odd, Yoshi thought, but for the first time in his life, he felt as if he were moving *toward* something rather than running *away*.

43

UNDER THE BLOSSOMS

Under the blossoms

utter strangers

simply don't exist

—Issa

Yoshi woke to the sound of the boat scraping along a pier. Dawn was just beginning to break. He stumbled off the boat to find himself, along with Jack and Manjiro, standing

A cherry tree grove. (*Ando Hiroshige*)

in a quiet grove of flowering cherry trees. Jack and Manjiro continued to chatter in that strange language that sounded like nonsense syllables to Yoshi. Otherwise, it was quiet.

Manjiro handed Yoshi the bundle of Jack's American clothes and shoes, and told Yoshi in Japanese, and Jack in English, what was to happen: The two boys were to wait for some of the stableboys, who would arrive shortly with a kago. They should be able to reach Kanagawa in time.

"In time for what?" Jack asked.

"For the banquet," Manjiro explained.

Jack glanced at Yoshi. So the little rascal had understood all along, he thought.

Jack's scolding glance did not escape Yoshi. He grinned sheepishly and tried that gesture that Manjiro made sometimes—that little lift of the shoulders.

Manjiro said it was time for him to take his leave. Yoshi watched him shake hands with Jack; it looked almost natural when they did it. He could *almost* understand it as a ritual of greeting or of parting. Then Manjiro turned to Yoshi, who bowed and held Manjiro's katana in his two extended hands, palms up, offering it to its owner.

But Manjiro shook his head. "Not yet," he said. "Who knows? You might still have need of it." He stepped into the boat, and the boatman pushed off, heading back upriver.

Yoshi figured this was as close to being a bushi as he would ever get. After this adventure was over, he would return the katana and be, simply, Yoshi. And that, he thought, would be fine. Still, he thought, for one time in his life, he could practice with a real blade, before the boys arrived with the kago.

He pulled the katana from its scabbard and admired the way it gleamed in the sunlight, the way it received, reflected, and deflected the light. Could Japan do the same? he wondered. Could Japan receive, reflect, and reject the changes that were sure to come?

His country would have to be like water, Yoshi thought, able to turn itself into a single drop or a vast ocean. It would have to be as renewing as fire, as elusive as air. Like wind, both he and his country would have to strive to find the right path in the coming days and years.

Now he gave himself up to his practice: He lunged, twisted, turned, and spun. He was water running over stones. He was a leaf, spinning in the spring wind. He was fire. He was like everything and like nothing at all. He was air.

Jack turned his eyes up at the flickering leaves overhead and breathed in the scent of the flowering trees. It was so quiet. In the very early morning light, pale blossoms drifted down around him silent as snow. Peaceful. He thought of the sounds of an American harbor: the clang of metal and the shouts of hundreds of dock and ship workers, the rumble of carts and carriage wheels on the cobbled streets, the shrill scream of steam whistles, the metallic grating of capstans. He could hear none of that here. The breeze in the pines, the twitter of birds, the gentle lapping of water. Tranquil.

He had heard it said that Japan was like an oyster—to open it would be to kill it. *Maybe*, he thought. He supposed the country would surely change. It would never be again like it was right now.

Jack watched as Yoshi carved the air with that big sword, practicing his lunging and parrying. *Graceful*, he thought. Like an art form.

Perhaps this, too, would be lost with the coming of modern weapons.

One thing that would never be killed, he thought as he watched Yoshi, was the spirit of these people. He wanted to drink it in, to open his eyes wide and remember every moment: the long hike to Edo, the baseball game, even the fearful time with those fervent samurai, and this time under these blossoms. But he was so tired, he could not keep his eyes open.

44

"OH! SUSANNA"

We must be encountering rough seas, Jack thought, judging by the uncomfortable jostling, shifting, and banging he was experiencing. Any minute now, he expected the bosun's whistle, the shout for "All hands!" and the order to "Clew up and furl the main topgallant!" But no order came, and the tossing continued unabated.

Such a dream he'd had: filled with sword-wielding warriors, near escapes, and a fairyland of forests, lush valleys, wooded hills, and distant, misty mountains. He'd seen exotic temples and forbidden castles. His dream, he thought now, in his half-sleep state, had been so real. He had made a friend in his dream, and with his friend had many adventures, fading from memory already, like that distant mountain that hovered, sometimes visible, sometimes not, in the blue haze . . .

He woke and blinked open his eyes, the taste of persimmons still on his tongue. It was dark. Where, he wondered, were the lanterns swaying from the rafters? His snoring berth mates—where were they? The creaking ship timbers? The water "talking" against the side of the ship? Instead, he heard running footfalls, incoherent voices. He was, it seemed, surrounded by cloth walls, and he was being jounced up and down, sideways, jiggling and joggling.

Then he remembered. He was in a kago being carried to Kanagawa. He poked his head outside the cloth flap and took a look around. He was inside a box suspended from a long pole, and it was being carried by four lads, two in front, two in back. This explained the lurching and joggling.

But he only had time for a quick glance before Yoshi's face appeared. Yoshi shoved Jack back inside and pulled the flap down.

At last they stopped, and the cloth wall lifted. Was that a band he heard? Horns and clarinets? And was that "The Star-Spangled Banner" being played? Jack craned his neck and saw, through the trees, the familiar waterfront, the familiar boats, the familiar blue-jacketed sailors. It was as if the past few days had been a dream after all.

But then he looked down and saw the silly nightgown he was wearing, and realized he had fallen asleep and been carried the last miles to his destination.

Yoshi appeared and presented Jack with his clothes, neatly folded: his jacket, trousers, shoes, and stockings. Everything was there.

"*Watch*," Yoshi said in English. "*Boat*." He pointed toward the waterfront.

Jack poked his head out of the kago and saw the sailors and marines making their way toward the boats lining the shore. He'd have to hurry or he'd miss his ride again!

Changing clothes inside the kago was no easy feat, even if you weren't in a hurry. Here an arm and there a leg would stick out as he tried to get a limb into a pant leg or a jacket sleeve. Each time a bare leg emerged, he heard the tittering giggles of the boys. Ah well, he thought, they deserved something for carrying him all that way, even if it was only a laugh. He wished he had something to give them.

Then he had a thought: Buttons! He yanked the two that remained from his jacket and two from his trousers. He climbed out of the kago with one hand full of buttons and the other holding up his pants.

Bowing to the boys, he presented the buttons. "Er . . . dozo," he said, suddenly remembering a word he'd heard so many times the last few days.

Each boy took one and bowed several times, thanking him.

Jack bowed, too, but he let go of his waistband to do it, and his trousers fell down.

While the others howled with laughter, Hiko took off his cloth headband and offered it to Jack to cinch around his waist. Then the four boys scampered off to examine their gifts more closely.

While Jack was tying the headband around his trousers, Yoshi suddenly remembered something. He reached into his sleeve and took out the small item he had found by the chasm in the forest. He bowed, and presenting it to Jack with both hands, said, "*Button.*"

Jack indicated to Yoshi that he should keep it, and Yoshi bowed again, touching the button reverently to his forehead. Then Jack thought of something else he wanted to give Yoshi, and he reached into his pocket and pulled out the box of matches.

Yoshi accepted the gift and took Jack's hand in an awkward handshake. It was not terrible, this hand shaking, he thought. It was a straightforward way of expressing, well, friendship. Yes, Yoshi thought, they had become friends. What, he wondered, could he give Jack?

There was the coin Manjiro had given him for the ferry. It would have been enough for all five boys and the kago, too. But it was the only thing Yoshi had to give, and so he fished it out and, bowing again, offered it to Jack.

Jack took the offered coin and bowed to Yoshi, trying to put as much gratitude, admiration, humility, and friendship into the move as he could. Yes, Jack thought, they had become friends.

Yoshi gestured to the beach, where Jack's shipmates were now climbing into the boats. Jack found that he had to quickly wipe his nose and swipe away a tear before saying one last good-bye. Looking up, he saw that Yoshi's eyes were filled with tears, too.

Then he turned and ran down the hill toward the waiting boats.

On the way home, Yoshi, Hiko, Han, Shozo, and Enju took turns riding in or carrying the kago. Manjiro's sword went

Banquet for the Americans. (*Hideki*)

inside the kago, because Yoshi didn't want to carry it. When he got back to Edo, he would return the sword to its owner. He would put away his bamboo sword. What he thought he would do was ask his friend Manjiro to teach him the outsider's language. He would learn to read it, and with the brush he would learn to write it. He already knew a song that Manjiro had taught him, and he sang it now:

"Oh! Susanna, oh don't you cry for me. / I come from Alabama with a banjo on my knee." Yoshi sang the verse, first in English, then as translated by Manjiro: "It rained all night the day I left, / The weather was so dry. / The sun so hot, I froze to death, / Susanna, don't you—"

Hiko stopped him. "That can't be right. It doesn't make any sense," he said.

The other boys agreed.

"That's the way Manjiro taught me," Yoshi said.

"How can the weather be dry if it is raining?" Enju asked.

"It just shows you how ignorant those barbarians really are. If the sun is hot, you can't freeze to death," Hiko added.

"Is that the way it *is* in their country?" Shozo said. "Everything is backward? One can freeze from the sun, and the rain is dry?"

"Yoshi has it wrong!" Han squeaked. "He has got the words wrong."

"Maybe it's a kind of joke," Hiko suggested.

Yoshi just smiled. To him it was a song about the impossible. It was a hopeful, optimistic song in which the impossible comes true. And that, Yoshi thought, as he took a last long look across the bay at the Black Ships, seemed more and more possible all the time.

A NOTE FROM JACK SULLIVAN

June 1860, Washington, D.C.

The United States steam frigate Roanoke was telegraphed as off Sandy Hook, on her way to New York City, with the expected Japanese Embassy on board . . . She anchored at half-past seven and allowed the official to convey an order to proceed to Washington before coming to New York.

—*Washington Evening Star*, May 10, 1860

It has been seven years since I traveled to Japan with Perry. I don't mean to make it sound as if he and I were traveling companions—hardly that! I was a mere cabin boy and he a commodore. He spoke to me only once, when he gave me the assignment of carrying the letter from President Fillmore in our very first encounter with the people of Japan.

Years later, I would photograph him. He spoke pleasantly to me on that occasion, although I'm sure he had no recollection of our previous association.

I think of it now, however, because of a most curious

occurrence. I have, for several years, been working as a camera operator for Mr. Mathew Brady, the famous photographer. As Mr. Brady's eyesight is failing, I am more and more frequently called upon to do his work. Recently, he asked me to photograph a delegation from Japan—the first official delegation, in fact—newly arrived in Washington, D.C. The embassy consisted of seventy-seven samurai along with their attendants, servants, interpreters, and the like. It was my job to photograph the diplomats during their visit to the Navy Yard.

After I had set up the equipment and placed the chairs, I decided I would try to focus my camera and make sure all was ready before the ambassadors got settled.

Many of those present were high-ranking officials who were kept busy on a tour led by officers of our navy. I could hardly ask them to sit while I fiddled with the camera. But standing slightly off to the side was a young man of low rank, wearing simple clothing and, unlike most of the others, with no swords at his side.

"Excuse me," I said. "You, er, sit? Focus camera?" I tried to indicate the task before me by gesturing at the camera.

"Yes, of course," the young man replied, in quite good English.

"I apologize," I said, and gestured to the chair where I wished the man to sit. "I didn't realize you spoke English so well."

"No, no!" the young man protested. "My English not well at all!"

"Your English is excellent!" said I, tossing the cloth over my head.

As I twisted the brass knob, the young man's face came into focus, and with it a kind of funny feeling. There was something so familiar . . . something about the expression, the level gaze, a kind of fearlessness that I remembered . . . Oh, but I was probably just imagining it.

I pulled my head out from under the cloth and squinted across the distance between us. "Are you an interpreter for the delegation?" I asked.

The young man bobbed his head in a bow of acknowledgment. "A poor one, I am sorry."

"I doubt that."

"I'm sure I make a better sitting model for focus a camera." He paused. "I didn't say that correctly."

"Close enough. I know what you meant." I sat down and patted my pockets, looking for a match.

"May I offer you a light?" the interpreter asked, whereupon he reached into his sleeve and procured a box of matches, one of which he struck into flame. But my eye had caught the design on the box: three red stars in a row. Coincidence? I wondered. Well, the delegation had been in America for quite some time already and could have picked up any number of matchboxes. And anyway, there were many American items available in Japan by this time.

I glanced at the delegates. They hadn't yet finished their tour, and so I thought to offer my model a beverage. "Would you care for something cold to drink?" I asked him.

"Thank you," the Japanese man said.

"Cider? Or sarsaparilla?"

The man looked a little pained—like he either didn't know or didn't like either one.

An idea came to me. "We'll flip a coin," I said. I reached into my pocket and took out the Japanese coin I always carried—I guess I have always thought of it as a good-luck charm. I sent the coin spiraling into the air, caught it as it fell, and slapped it on the back of my hand, then showed the coin, still resting there, to the young interpreter.

He looked from the coin to my face, then reached into his sleeve and pulled out a button, and held it out to show me.

Then I knew: This was the same person I had met twice in Japan, with whom I had shared such an adventure.

"Yoshi?" I asked.

"Mr. Jack!" Yoshi said, bowing deeply.

I bowed, and we shook hands, both of us grinning like kids.

"This is a most amazing coincidence!" I exclaimed.

"Most remarkable!" Yoshi agreed.

I retrieved two bottles of sarsaparilla—never mind how the coin toss turned out—removed the caps, handed one to Yoshi, and sat down next to him.

"Friend of mine is experimenting with putting this stuff in bottles," I told him. "Ever tried it?"

Yoshi shook his head and looked at the bottle suspiciously.

"Well," I said. "Give it a try. If you don't like it, you don't have to drink it."

I tipped the bottle to my lips and gulped.

Yoshi followed suit, sipping hesitantly.

"How have you found America?" I asked him.

"It is a thing to make you dizzy," Yoshi said. "I don't know how to say."

"Dizzying," I said.

"Yes," said Yoshi. "People are very kind. There are many banquets and parades in our honor. I get the sense that Americans welcome us as an . . . entertainment. Like a music show or party. A diversion to take their minds away from something else. What is it Americans try so hard not to think about?"

"You are very perceptive," I said.

"Perceptive?"

"It means you see something most others would not."

"But I do not see," Yoshi said. "That is why I ask."

"You are probably right. People don't want to think about the trouble brewing," I said. "Trouble between slaveholding states and free states. There is talk that slaveholding states will secede from the United States."

"And make their own country?"

"Yes," I said.

"What will happen then?"

I shook my head. "Some say there will be war."

"I am sorry to hear it," Yoshi said.

"There is trouble in your country, too, we have heard," I told him. "News has just arrived here by pony express from San Francisco about events in Japan."

"Oh?" Yoshi said. "What has happened?"

"We have heard through Ambassador Harris that there has been turmoil in Japan since you've been away. Violence."

"Please tell me."

I lowered my voice and said, "A high-level councillor of the government, Lord I or Lord Ee or something like that."

"Lord Ii?" Yoshi whispered. He pronounced it *Ee-ay*.

"That's right." I glanced over my shoulder. "He was murdered! Cut down by a group of assassins in the street—

in the middle of a snowstorm! Apparently the anti-foreign movement is gaining momentum. 'Repel the Barbarians, Revere the Emperor!' That's their rallying cry."

I glanced at Yoshi, who looked as stricken as that time he knew he'd have to cross the log over the river.

"Apparently they pledge to kill the Westerners and any of their own countrymen who associate with them," I told him. "Even those who study English or use American-made items."

Yoshi nodded numbly. I could see he was pondering what this meant for their delegation when they returned home.

"And we say that your countrymen are barbarians," Yoshi said. "But people in your country don't murder their leaders. Can you imagine someone killing your president?"

"No," I said.

"Has it ever happened?"

"No, and I hope it will never happen," I answered. "But it seems we are both looking at troubled times for our countries."

"Indeed," Yoshi agreed. Then he cleared his throat and went on. "But, however, I am happy to meet you again. I have always wanted to thank you for what you did for me in the forest long ago. You saved my life!"

"And you saved mine!" I said.

Tears came to the young interpreter's eyes, and I pulled

out a handkerchief and gave it to him. "You don't want to have bleary eyes for the photograph, do you?"

"Oh, I won't be in photograph," he said. "Only officials. I am only humble servant."

"To me, my friend," I said, "you are as noble as a samurai."

Yoshi smiled a little and tipped his head, acknowledging the compliment.

We sat there for some moments more, and although you may be thinking that this odd coincidence—two people from across the world finding each other again this way—that this is what I meant when I said a curious thing happened, that is actually not quite what I meant.

As we sat there, chatting amiably, it felt to me as if we were old friends. Even more than friends—brothers. This is strange, don't you think? To have found a brother in such a faraway place? But perhaps we are not so terribly distant after all.

The first official Japanese delegation to America. (*Matthew Brady*)

AUTHOR'S NOTE

One of our sailors charmed with the Robinson Crusoe like life of the Island has deserted. He has not been heard from for several days, and some think he has fallen from one of the cliffs and got killed. If not, hunger must soon drive him to seek the ship again. He was a likely lad, and we regret his making a fool of himself.

—from Lieutenant George Henry Preble's diary

Although a sailor did briefly desert as indicated in the above diary entry, there's no indication that a cabin boy named Jack jumped ship while the Black Ships were anchored off Kanagawa (in present-day Yokohama). In fact, Jack's and Yoshi's adventures are largely fictional. The historical events they live through and many of the people they encounter, however, are very real.

THE REAL EVENTS

On July 8, 1853, four black American steamships appeared in Edo Bay (Edo is the present-day Tokyo). This was in spite of the shogun's edict forbidding foreigners to enter Japanese waters or to set foot on Japanese soil. The Americans entered with bold confidence in ships that could move without sails, puffed out black smoke, and bristled with cannon and other modern weaponry.

The affront threw Japan into an uproar. Preparations were made for war, edicts were issued, and requests were sent to the Americans to move their ships. But the Americans, under the command of Com-

Commodore Matthew Perry. (*Matthew Brady*)

modore Matthew Calbraith Perry, refused to budge, insisting instead on delivering a letter from the president of the United States to the mikado, which is what they called the emperor. The Americans didn't realize they would be dealing with the shogun and the ruling body, called the Bakufu, and not with the emperor.

Perry promised to return one year later with the intent of signing a treaty to open some Japanese ports to American interests. Merchant steamships wanted coal; whalers wanted a place to resupply; and the United States wanted to be the first to set up a trading partnership with the country.

Japan, known to its own people as Nippon, had been living in isolation for the previous 250 years. After expelling Portuguese and Spanish missionaries from Japan in 1610, the shogun continued to isolate the country, only allowing a handful of Dutch merchants to continue trade with Japan by confining them to the small, man-made island of Dejima.

During this period, Japan lived in peace and had little interest in opening to Western powers, which it perceived as bullying and warlike, with a conquering mentality. There was basis for this belief: While Japan was quietly refining arts such as woodblock printing, flower arrangement, poetry, drama, textiles, and cuisine, the Western world had been extremely busy killing and conquering one another. During this same 250-year period in the West, the number of wars that took place are too long to list here, but they include just about any combination of countries you can imagine. The American Revolution, the French Revolution, and the Napoleonic Wars were just a few of the many conflicts that raged during this time.

Naturally, all this warring resulted in advances in military technology and weaponry—advances from which Japan did not benefit. Having lived for so long in isolation, the Japanese knew very little about the outside world. All foreigners were considered barbarians, and stories abounded regarding their strangeness. It was believed that the foreigners could see in the dark, couldn't bend their legs, and stank from eating flesh (which was probably true, actually). Prints of the day showed barbarians with holes in their chests, or with only one eye, or with arms that dragged on the ground.

The Americans had equally misguided opinions about the Japanese. Perry himself considered them "a weak and barbarous people," and opinions among others varied from thinking them "the most polite people on the face of the earth" to no more than "savages, liars, a pack of fools." (Quotations throughout the author's note have been taken from the sources that are marked with asterisks in the bibliography, which starts on page 325.)

Only seven months after he left Japan, Perry returned, this time with eight ships, and demanded that a treaty be signed. Completed on March 31, 1854, the Treaty of Kanagawa granted the Americans two trading ports, Shimoda and Hakodate.

Debates raged throughout Japan about the best way to move forward. Was it better to rid the country of the foreigners now, or to learn from them and then kick them out? Was it time to rid the country of the shogun and reinstate the emperor as the supreme ruler? Or was there another, different way to rule the country?

Many of the characters in this story are based on the real people who carried on these debates.

The United States of America, and the Empire of Japan, desiring to establish firm lasting and sincere friendship between the two Nations, have resolved to fix in a manner clear and positive, by means of a Treaty or general convention of peace and Amity, the rules which shall in future be mutually observed in the intercourse of their respective Countries; for which most desirable object, the President of the United States has conferred full powers on his Commissioner, Matthew Calbraith Perry, Special Ambassador of the United States to Japan: And the August Sovereign of Japan has given similar full powers to his Commissioners, Hayashi, Dai-gaku no-Kami; Ido, Prince of Tsus-Sima; Izawa, Prince of Mima-saki; and Udono, Member of the Board of Revenue. And the said Commissioners after having exchanged their said full powers, and duly considered the premises, have agreed to the following Articles.

Part of the Treaty of Kanagawa.

THE REAL PEOPLE

Note: Japanese names are here recorded in Japanese fashion—surname first.

NAKAHAMA MANJIRO (1827–98). Manjiro was fourteen years old when he and his four fishing companions were blown away from the coast of Japan by a storm. After being shipwrecked on an island far from Japan, they were rescued by an American whaling ship. Manjiro and the captain of that ship, William Whitfield, became such good friends that Whitfield took Manjiro back to America with him to live as his son. An excellent student, Manjiro studied English, mathematics, and modern methods of navigation, unknown in Japan at the time. He also became a first-rate sailor and learned much about ships and the sea. After several years of adventure, during which he sailed on whalers and took part in the California gold rush, he made his way back to Japan with

Undated portrait of Nakahama Manjiro, circa 1877. (*artist unknown*)

two of his previous companions. They were promptly arrested and held in a kind of house arrest for two years.

Many of the things about America that Manjiro tells Yoshi, the men from the bath, or the Bakufu's officials are nearly direct quotes of what he told his interrogators and the shogun's advisers. During the summer of 1852, he told his story to Kawada Shoryo, who recorded it in a book titled *Hyoson kiryaku* (later translated into English as *Drifting Toward the Southeast*; see page 309). Manjiro introduced many American ideas and concepts to Japan, including the country's motto, "E pluribus unum."

Shortly after Manjiro's release, Commodore Perry arrived with his fleet, and Manjiro was summoned to Edo to advise the shogun. He also became the official curator of Commodore Perry's gifts, being probably the only person in Japan who could name and interpret them! Not everyone trusted him, however, believing he might have been a spy for the Americans, and he was never allowed to have direct contact with members of the expedition. His counsel, however, likely influenced the shogun and the Bakufu to open Japan peacefully to the West.

Manjiro was given samurai status and allowed to carry the daisho, but when he was first given the two swords, he bundled them in a towel to carry them home. He was also known (later in life) to give away his restaurant leftovers to beggars.

During his lifetime, Manjiro taught English to young

samurai, translated Nathaniel Bowditch's *New American Practical Navigator* into Japanese, and oversaw the building and sailing of a whaling ship, among many other accomplishments. In 1860, he accompanied the first official Japanese delegation as far as San Francisco, serving as an interpreter for the eleven U.S. Navy crewmen who were aboard the *Kanrin Maru*. Manjiro and the American crew are credited with successfully bringing the ship through storms and heavy seas.

History does not indicate that he ever hired an "apprentice bodyguard" or that he had a young friend like Yoshi. Although it is believed that attempts may have been made on his life, the one described in this story is entirely fictional.

You can read more about Manjiro's early life in my book *Heart of a Samurai*.

SHISHI, OR LOYALISTS. The "soba shop samurai" in this story are fictional characters, but they are based on young idealists of the time who became known as "shishi," or loyalists—loyal to the emperor, desirous of overthrowing the shogun. Over time, many of these young, generally lower-rank samurai, sometimes ronin (meaning masterless, so sort of a freelance samurai), were responsible for the transformation of Japan's government. These passionate young men met in tea and sake houses to discuss the future of their country.

SAKAMOTO RYOMA (1836–67) was only sixteen years old when Perry's steamships arrived in Japanese waters. He was a promising swordsman and a student at Chiba Dojo in Edo when he and his classmates were assigned military duty following Perry's first landing. Like many of his countrymen, he shared the impression that war was imminent. "I think there will be a war soon," he wrote to his father in October 1853. "If it comes to that, you can be sure I will cut off a foreign head before coming home."

At first staunchly antiforeign, Sakamoto joined others who believed in assassinating foreigners, as well as Japanese who seemed to be sympathetic to them. He targeted Katsu Rintaro (also known as Katsu Kaishu), a high-ranking official in the Tokugawa shogunate, who was a supporter of modernization and Westernization. Sakamoto entered Katsu's home with the intention of killing him, but Katsu talked him out of it, explaining his plan to strengthen Japan's defenses and military. After their conversation, Sakamoto became Katsu's protégé; together they helped modernize the Japanese navy.

Sakamoto Ryoma was also the creator of an eight-point plan that served as the basis of the new Japanese government. He came to support the idea of modernizing and was inspired by the example of the United States, where "all men are created equal." His style reflected his sensibilities, and he was often seen wearing Western-style shoes with traditional samurai clothing. He proved to be such a skillful negotiator among warring factions in the country that he is known as the "Benjamin Franklin of Japan."

He was murdered on his birthday in 1867, at the age of thirty-one, in Kyoto.

YOSHIDA SHOIN (1830–59) emerged as a leading spokesman of the shishi movement. He studied with idealists such as Sakuma Zozan and Aizawa Seishisai (page 308). Intensely antiforeign, Yoshida wrote extensively about the danger of allowing Westerners into the country. Among many other things, he said, "It is clear that the Americans' intentions are harmful to the Land of the Gods [Japan]. . . . The words of the American envoy have caused the Land of the Gods to be dishonored."

At one point, he and his friends briefly discussed a plot to assassinate Perry, but, deciding it would do more harm than good, they abandoned the plan. Yoshida came around to espouse his mentor Sakuma's idea that to "drive off the barbarians, the first thing to do is to learn their ways."

That belief motivated him and a colleague to travel to Shimoda, where the Black Ships anchored after the treaty was signed in 1854. There they asked to be taken to America. Their written request to the Americans stated, "We have been for many years desirous of going over the 'five great continents,' but the laws of our country are very strict; for foreigners to come into the country, and for natives to go abroad, are both immutably forbidden. . . . Happily the arrival of your ships in these waters has revived the thoughts of many years and they are urgent for an exit."

Perry rejected their application, not wanting to jeopardize the recently signed treaty, and the two men were sent back to shore with a request from Perry that they be treated kindly. Nonetheless, they were arrested and locked in bamboo cages, by which they were transported to prison in Edo. (These are the men whom Yoshi and Jack see as they travel to Edo together.)

One and a half years later, Yoshida was released from prison, after which he continued to work for a transformed government. He was imprisoned again and finally executed in 1859.

Yoshida's teacher SAKUMA ZOZAN (1811–64), also called Sakuma Shozan, was also highly nationalistic but responded differently to the idea of Western intrusion. He favored opening Japan's doors in order to gain certain aspects of Western knowledge. "To drive off the barbarians," he said, "the first thing that must be done is to understand their ways. To understand their ways, the most important thing is to become familiar with their language." He argued that in those things concerning "morality, benevolence, and righteousness," among other matters, his countrymen should "follow the examples and precepts of the Chinese sages." However, in the sciences, construction, and "the art of gunnery," they should rely on the West. "We must gather the strong points of the five worlds," he said, "and construct the great learning of our imperial nation."

Sakuma was killed in Kyoto by an antiforeign zealot in 1864.

AIZAWA SEISHISAI (1781–1863) of Mito was one of the earliest advocates of the policy of "sonno joi" (revere the emperor; expel the barbarians). Aizawa held Japan to be "at the vertex of the earth," the nation that set the standard for others to follow. He was an influential teacher of many of the loyalists, and he wrote, "Today the alien barbarians of the West, lowly organs of the legs and feet of the world, are dashing about across the sea, trampling other countries underfoot, and daring, with their squinting eyes and limping feet, to override the noble nations. What manner of arrogance is this! . . . Our divine land is situated at the top of the earth. . . . America occupies the hindmost region of the earth; thus, its people are stupid and simple, and are incapable of doing things."

KAWADA SHORYO also influenced these loyalists. He wrote *Hyoson kiryaku*, an account of the experiences of Nakahama Manjiro. From his encounters with Manjiro, he became a source of information about the West to young, curious samurai, including Sakamoto Ryoma.

Kawada's account is available in English, translated by Junya Nagakuni and Junji Kitadai and titled *Drifting Toward the Southeast*.

FUKUZAWA YUKICHI (1834–1901) became the "outstanding popularizer of Western knowledge in nineteenth century Japan." He was one of the private servants who served under the commander of the *Kanrin Maru*. Along with Manjiro, Fukuzawa visited San Francisco in 1860, where they each procured a copy of a Webster's dictionary. "Once I had secured this valuable work," Fukuzawa would later write in his autobiography, "I felt no disappointment on leaving the new world and returning home."

Fukuzawa is the founder of Keio University, the oldest institute of higher education in Japan.

THE GREAT LORDS, DAIMYO, COUNCILLORS, AND OTHER OFFICIALS

TOKUGAWA IEYOSHI (1793–1853) was the twelfth shogun of the Tokugawa shogunate. Shortly after Perry arrived, he died and was succeeded by his son TOKUGAWA IESADA (1824–58).

EGAWA TAROZAEMON (1801–55), chief secretary of the Department of Navigation, Survey, and Shipbuilding, took great interest in Manjiro and let him live on the premises of his yashiki (mansion) in Edo. He was appointed as a sort of "foreign minister" to deal with the Americans and asked that Manjiro be his interpreter. As in this story, however, other high-ranking officials, notably Tokugawa Nariaki and Abe Masahiro (see below), disagreed with this proposal.

TOKUGAWA NARIAKI (1800–60), Lord of Mito, was fanatically antiforeign and, with family ties to both the Tokugawa family and the emperor, a powerful leader.

The Lord of Mito had many negative things to say about the

West, including this: "The barbarians have been watching our country with greedy eyes for many years . . . If we are frightened now by their aggressive lying strategies and give them what they ask for . . . they will manage bit by bit to impoverish the country; after which they will treat us just as they like; perhaps behave with the greatest rudeness and insult us, and end by swallowing up Japan. If we don't drive them away now, we shall never have another opportunity."

He argued in favor of war with the Americans, saying, "If we put our trust in war the whole country's morale will be increased and even if we sustain an initial defeat we will in the end expel the foreigner." He also said, "In these feeble days men tend to cling to peace; they are not fond of defending their country by war."

In arguing against Manjiro being an interpreter at the treaty signing, Nariaki wrote: "There was once a dragon tamed and domesticated that one day drove through wind and cloud in the midst of a hurricane and took flight. Once that man changed his mind and was taken away on an American ship it would be to repent too late."

ABE MASAHIRO (1819–57), chief senior councillor of the shogunate, also expressed an opinion regarding Manjiro's reliability, saying, "I do not think that Manjiro has any thoughts of treason, but upon getting on board that ship, there is no telling what might happen. Considering the fact that Manjiro was taken to America by that foreigner, we do not know what method he might use in talking to the men on the ships."

II NAOSUKE (1815–60), daimyo of Hikone, was in favor of signing a treaty with Perry to avoid military conflict. He believed that forestalling the foreigners was the best method of "ensuring that the Bakufu will at some future time find opportunity to reimpose its ban and forbid foreigners to come to Japan." He was a supporter and sponsor of the delegation to America, but he was assassinated shortly after the delegates sailed in 1860. His murder signaled a surge of antiforeign sentiment.

The imperial family, including EMPEROR KOMEI (1831–67), whose lineage extended to the "dawn of time," had not had any meaningful ruling power in Japan since 1603, when the shogun Tokugawa Ieyasu united the country under his rule.

The arrival of the Black Ships and the chaos that ensued— and the obvious inability of the shogun to expel them—gave the emperor a perfect opportunity to assert his authority. The loyalist faction believed that reinstating the emperor on the throne was needed to get the country back on the right track. The emperor took advantage of the antiforeign feeling to make statements aimed at embarrassing the shogun. He said that "friendship with foreigners will be a stain upon it [Japan], and an insult to the first Mikado. It will be an everlasting shame for the country to be afraid of those foreigners, and for us to bear patiently their arbitrary and rough manners; and the time will come when we shall be subservient to them."

THE ARTISTS

Although the artist, Ozawa, is a fictional character, the artist whose story he tells, SESSHU TOYO (1420–1506), was one of the greatest Japanese artists of his era. As a boy, he studied Zen Buddhism at a temple where the story of the rats (or mice, or cats) was born. A variant of the story was written in English by Lafcadio Hearn in 1897 and is also told in more recent picture books, *The Boy Who Drew Cats*, by Margaret Hodges, and another by Arthur A. Levine with the same title.

Two famous wood-block artists of the time who are still well-known today are Ando Hiroshige (1797–1858) and Katsushika Hokusai (1760–1849), both of whom traveled the country making pictures of everyday life on the Tokaido and in Edo. Much of the art depicted in this book was created by artists who were alive during this period; some may even have witnessed the events described here.

THE REAL PEOPLE ON THE EXPEDITION

Many of the statements by characters in the chapters "Aboard the *Susquehanna*," "The Comet," and "The Lark" are taken from the journals and letters of the following members of the expedition:

WILLIAM B. ALLEN: a cabin boy

LIEUTENANT SILAS BENT: in regard to bowing, the lieutenant expressed his determination "that no such obsequiousness should be shown on the deck of an American man-of-war, and under the flag of the United States, to anything wearing the human form . . ."

WILHEM "WILLIAM" HEINE: the expedition's artist

JOHN R. C. LEWIS: the master's mate

LIEUTENANT GEORGE HENRY PREBLE: a deck officer aboard the sloop of war *Macedonian*

WILLIAM SPEIDEN JR.: the purser's son and assistant

S. WELLS WILLIAMS: one of the expedition's interpreters

COMMODORE MATHEW CALBRAITH PERRY (1794–1858) insisted on being called "Admiral" during the negotiations, believing it would heighten his prestige. He avoided direct contact with any but the highest-level Japanese officials, and every public appearance he made a formal ceremony. He was known as the Tycoon, the American Mikado, and probably many less favorable names by the Japanese.

Officially, the expedition's goal was to establish a trading partnership with Japan; however, this was the era of "Manifest Destiny," the popular nineteenth-century belief that it was the destiny of the United States to expand its territory over the entirety of North America (and possibly beyond), and Perry may have believed that he was obeying a moral imperative in seeking to bring Japan within the family of nations. In the phrase of the day, "The time of God's working had come."

The character of JACK SULLIVAN is inspired (very slightly) by TIMOTHY O'SULLIVAN (1840–82), who became one of the world's first war correspondents, taking many photographs of the Civil War, and later of the western United States. The famous photographer Mathew Brady was asked to be the official photographer of the 1860 Japanese delegation, and he—or, since his eyesight was failing by this time, one of his camera operators—took the photograph at the Washington Navy Yard (see pages 294–95). O'Sullivan would have been twenty years old in 1860, making him, like Jack, thirteen in 1853. Even though very little is known about his early life, it is unlikely that he traveled on any navy ship anywhere, including to Japan.

GLOSSARY

JAPANESE TERMS

bushi (or samurai): a warrior

daimyo: the provincial lord; literally, "great name"

daisho: the samurai's two swords, katana and wakizashi, worn together; katana is the long sword, and wakizashi the short sword (primarily for the purpose of seppuku)

dojo: a practice hall for kendo or other martial arts

dozo: "Please" or "Here you go" or "Help yourself"

Fuji-san: the highest mountain in Japan, located about sixty miles southwest of Tokyo (Edo)

fuki-leaf: the large downy leaf of the giant butterbur, a perennial shrub

kamikaze: literally, "divine wind"; the storms that destroyed invading Mongol fleets in 1274 and again in 1281

katana: see daisho

kendo: "the Way of the Sword"; a Japanese martial art that uses bamboo swords

koban: a gold coin of significant value

lacquer: sap of the lacquer tree, used as a smooth, varnish-like finish for wood or other materials

mikado: the emperor of Japan

ronin: a samurai who no longer served a lord

sake: rice wine

seppuku (or hara-kiri—literally, "belly slicing"): ritual suicide

shakkei: the principle of incorporating background landscape into the composition of a garden

shogun: a commander in chief; literally, "barbarian-suppressing generalissimo"

shoji: a traditional Japanese door, window, or room divider made of paper over a wood frame

soba: buckwheat; buckwheat noodle

sutra: a Buddhist text or prayer

tatami: rice-straw mats used for flooring in traditional Japanese homes

tengu: a goblin or devil that has a bird's wings or head and a long nose

Tokaido (East Sea Road): the major road in Edo-period Japan, connecting Edo (present-day Tokyo) to Kyoto and running along the coast

wakizashi: see daisho

SHIPBOARD AND MILITARY TERMS

aloft: up in the tops, at the mastheads or anywhere in the higher rigging

avast: "Stop!" "Cease!" in shipboard parlance

battery: a land-based military fortification containing heavy guns

bosun (boatswain or bos'n): the officer responsible for handling the crew and for the ship's general maintenance; he piped orders to the crew with a pipe or whistle

bulwark: planking around the edge of the upper deck, which stops the sea from washing over the decks and prevents members of the crew from being swept overboard in high seas

capstan: apparatus enabling the anchor to be raised by hand

carbine: a short, light musket (or rifle)

carronade: a short-barreled cannon that fires large shot at short range

"clew up": to haul the lower corners (the "clews") of a square sail up to the yard by means of the clew lines

companionway: a stairway or ladder leading from the deck to the accommodations below

cutlass: a short, heavy sword with a curved blade used by sailors on war vessels

deadeye: a round or pear-shaped wooden block used in the standing rigging to create purchase for a shroud (rope supporting the mast)

deadlight: a circular piece of thick ground glass inserted into the deck to give light below

gaskets: short lines attached to the yard used to secure a furled sail

halyard: rope or lines used to hoist or lower sails

marlinspike: an iron pin, about sixteen inches long and tapered to a point; used to separate the strands of a rope when splicing

powder magazine: the storeroom on a man-of-war in which gunpowder and explosives are kept

rail: the upper edge of the bulwarks

ratlines: steps made out of rope or wood attached to the shrouds, that allow the sailors to climb into the rigging

reef (reefing sails): to reduce sail area by gathering up part of the sail

sails: the Black Ships were powered by both steam and sail; the sails mentioned in the story include main topgallant, skysail, and topsails (all topmost sails)

shot: cannon ammunition; kinds mentioned in the story are grape shot (so called because of its resemblance to a cluster of grapes on the vine) and canister shot (small iron shot or lead musket balls contained in a metal can that breaks up when fired)

64-pounder: a muzzle-loading cannon

slush bucket: a bucket containing a mixture of linseed oil and tallow soap, used to grease masts to allow easier movement for the running gear

spar: a long wooden timber or pole used as a yard (see below) or a mast

splicing hammer: a hammer tapered at one end, used in splicing

squilgee: another name for a squeegee, used to push water from the deck surface after it has been cleaned

yard: a horizontal wooden boom (or spar) to which sail is attached

MISCELLANEOUS TERMS

bannermen: the forerunners of a great lord or daimyo who carried the banners imprinted with the family crest in the lord's processions

Daguerreotype apparatus: an early camera (a large box, sometimes on legs)

fetlocks: cushion-like protection on the back of a horse's leg, above the hoof

SELECTED BIBLIOGRAPHY

Benedict, Ruth. *The Chrysanthemum and the Sword: Patterns of Japanese Culture.* Boston: Houghton Mifflin, 1946.

Bird, Isabella L. *Unbeaten Tracks in Japan.* Mineola, N.Y.: Dover, 2005. Originally published in 1911.

* Blumberg, Rhoda. *Commodore Perry in the Land of the Shogun.* New York: Lothrop, Lee & Shepard Books, 1985.

Bush, Lewis. *77 Samurai: Japan's First Embassy to America.* Tokyo: Kodansha International, 1968.

Chamberlain, Basil Hall. *Japanese Things: Being Notes on Various Subjects Connected with Japan.* Rutland, Vt.: Charles E. Tuttle, 1971.

Craig, Darrell. *Iai-Jitsu: Center of the Circle.* Rutland, Vt.: Charles E. Tuttle, 1981.

* *Quotations that appear in the Author's Note have been taken from these sources.*

Deal, William E. *Handbook to Life in Medieval and Early Modern Japan*. New York: Oxford University Press, 2006.

Dock, George, Jr. *Audubon's Birds of America*. New York: Arrowood, 1987.

* Dulles, Foster Rhea. *Yankees and Samurai: America's Role in the Emergence of Modern Japan, 1791–1900*. New York: Harper & Row, 1965.

Dunn, C. J. *Everyday Life in Traditional Japan*. New York: G. P. Putnam's Sons, 1969.

* Duus, Peter. *The Japanese Discovery of America: A Brief History with Documents*. Boston: Bedford Books, 1997.

* Earle, David Magarey Earl. *Emperor and Nation in Japan: Political Thinkers of the Tokugawa Period*. Seattle, Wash.: University of Washington Press. 1964.

Guth, Christine. *Art of Edo Japan: The Artist and the City, 1615–1868*. New York: Harry N. Abrams, 1996.

* Hane, Mikiso. *Premodern Japan: A Historical Survey*. Boulder, Colo.: Westview, 1991.

Hearn, Lafcadio. *Japan: An Attempt at Interpretation*. Rutland, Vt.: Charles E. Tuttle, 1955. Originally published in 1904.

Hillsborough, Romulus. *Ryoma: Life of a Renaissance Samurai*. San Francisco: Ridgeback, 1999.

Horan, James D. *Timothy O'Sullivan: America's Forgotten Photographer*. New York: Bonanza Books, 1966.

* Jansen, Marius B. *Sakamoto Ryōma and the Meiji Restoration*. Stanford, Calif.: Stanford University Press, 1971.

Kaneko, Hisakazu. *Manjiro, the Man Who Discovered America*. Boston: Houghton Mifflin, 1956.

Katsu Kokichi. *Musui's Story: The Autobiography of a Tokugawa Samurai*. Translated by Teruko Craig. Tucson: University of Arizona Press, 1988.

Lehmann, Jean-Pierre. *The Roots of Modern Japan.* New York: St. Martin's Press, 1982.

Leupp, Gary P. *Servants, Shophands, and Laborers in the Cities of Tokugawa Japan.* Princeton, N.J.: Princeton University Press, 1992.

Melville, Herman. *Redburn: His First Voyage. . . .* Edited by Harold Beaver. New York: Penguin Books, 1976. Originally published in 1849.

———. *White-Jacket; or, The World in a Man-of-War.* Evanston, Ill.: Northwestern University Press, 2000. Originally published in 1850.

Miyamoto Musashi. *A Book of Five Rings: The Classic Guide to Strategy.*

* Miyoshi, Masao. *As We Saw Them: The First Japanese Embassy to the United States.* Philadelphia: Paul Dry Books, 2005.

Najita, Tetsuo. *Japan: The Intellectual Foundations of Modern Japanese Politics.* Chicago: University of Chicago Press, 1974.

Nakae Chōmin. *A Discourse by Three Drunkards on Government.* Translated by Nobuko Tsukui. New York: Weatherhill, 1984. Originally published in 1887.

Nakahama, Kyo. *John Manjiro; The Starting Point of Friendship Between Japan and the United States.* JASRAC. Printed in Japan. 2008.

Place, François. *The Old Man Mad About Drawing: A Tale of Hokusai.* Translated by William Rodarmor. Boston: David R. Godine, 2001.

* Plummer, Katherine. *The Shogun's Reluctant Ambassadors: Sea Drifters.* Tokyo: Lotus, 1984.

* Statler, Oliver. *The Black Ship Scroll: An Account of the Perry Expedition at Shimoda in 1854* . . . Tokyo: John Weatherhill, 1963.

Sugimoto, Etsu Inagaki. *A Daughter of the Samurai.* Garden City, N.Y.: Doubleday, Doran, 1928.

Turnbull, Stephen R. *The Book of the Samurai, the Warrior Class of Japan.* New York: Galler Books, 1982.

———. *Samurai: The Story of Japan's Great Warriors*. London: PRC, 2004.

The Visual Encyclopedia of Nautical Terms Under Sail. New York: Crown, 1978.

* Walworth, Arthur. *Black Ships off Japan: The Story of Commodore Perry's Expedition*. New York: Alfred A. Knopf, 1946.

Warinner, Emily V. *Voyager to Destiny*. Indianapolis: Bobbs-Merrill, 1956.

Yamamoto Tsunetomo. *Hagakure: The Book of the Samurai*. Translated by William Scott Wilson. Tokyo: Kodansha International, 1979.

DIARIES AND
FIRST-PERSON ACCOUNTS

* Graff, Henry F., ed. *Bluejackets with Perry in Japan: A Day-by-Day Account Kept by Master's Mate John R. C. Lewis and Cabin Boy William B. Allen*. New York: New York Public Library, 1952.

* Heine, William. *With Perry to Japan: A Memoir by William Heine.* Translated by Frederic Trautmann. Honolulu: University of Hawaii Press, 1990. Originally published in 1856.

* Manjiro, John, and Kawada Shoryo. *Drifting Toward the Southeast: The Story of Five Japanese Castaways.* Translated by Junya Nagakuni and Junji Kitadai. New Bedford, Mass.: Spinner, 2003.

Perry, Commodore M. C. *Narrative of the Expedition to the China Seas and Japan, 1852–1854.* Mineola, N.Y.: Dover, 2000. Originally published in 1856.

* Preble, George Henry. *The Opening of Japan: A Diary of Discovery in the Far East, 1853–1856.* Edited by Boleslaw Szczesniak. Norman: University of Oklahoma Press, 1962.

* Wolter, John A., David A. Ranzan, and John J. McDonough, eds. *With Commodore Perry to Japan: The Journal of William Speiden Jr., 1852–1855.* Annapolis, Md.: Naval Institute Press, 2013.

ILLUSTRATION CREDITS

Title page: Yuko Shimizu. Pages v–ix: Yuko Shimizu. Page 9: Public domain. Page 18: Yuko Shimizu. Page 22: Yuko Shimizu. Pages 40–41: Courtesy of the Historiographical Institute, University of Tokyo. Page 48: Courtesy of the Honolulu Museum of Art. Pages 52–53: Courtesy of the Rijksmuseum, Amsterdam. Page 63: Public domain. Page 66: Courtesy of the Honolulu Museum of Art. Page 73: Wikimedia Commons. Page 80: Wikimedia Commons. Page 84: Wikimedia Commons. Page 92: Courtesy of the Honolulu Museum of Art. Page 114: Public domain. 124: Public domain. Pages 142–43: Author's collection. Page 146: Public domain. Page 148: Public domain. Pages 172–73: Wikimedia Commons. Page 182: Public domain. Page 200: Public domain. Page 210: Public domain. Page 224: Library of Congress LC-DIG-jpd-02398. Page 235: Wikimedia Commons. Page 264: Yuko Shimizu. Page 275: Library of Congress LC-DIG-jpd-00507. Page 283: Courtesy of the Brooklyn Museum Collection. Pages 294–95: Public domain. Page 298: Library of Congress LC-H261-2000137. Page 301: US National Archives, Record Group 11. Page 302: Public domain.

ACKNOWLEDGMENTS

I had a lot to learn in order to write this book, and I owe much to the wise counsel, sage advice, and expertise of the following people: Junji Kitadai, Eri Fujieda, Bob Bruce, Peter Bleed, Ryuta Nakajima, Peter Duus, Catherine Preus, Maryann Weidt, and Miaki Habuka and David Hammer.

Special thanks to Stephen Salel of the Honolulu Museum of Art for the opportunity to see the Black Ship Scroll and for his insights into its history and significance, and for permission to use images from the scroll.

Thanks to illustrator Yuko Shimizu for the exciting art and to my agent, Stephen Fraser, for encouragement. An enormous *arigato gozaimasu* to the brilliant people at Abrams/Amulet: Chad Beckerman and Melissa Arnst, Elizabeth Peskin, Richard Slovak, Jim Armstrong, Jason Wells, and especially Howard Reeves, whose sparkly red pen is, indeed, mightier than the sword.

Lastly, thanks to Miori Dejima for asking the question that set me off on this adventure.

ABOUT THE AUTHOR

Margi Preus is the author of the Newbery Honor winner *Heart of a Samurai* as well as the highly praised novels *Shadow on the Mountain* and *West of the Moon*. She has traveled the globe to research her books and, along the way, made friends in Japan, Norway, and many other places. She lives in Duluth, Minnesota. Visit her online at margipreus.com

READER'S GUIDE

1. This story is told by two narrators: Yoshi and Jack. Why do you think the author decided to write the book this way? How are the two narrators' perspectives similar? How are their perspectives different?

2. Though Yoshi wants to be a bushi, he is not allowed to train as a samurai because he was born into the wrong class. Do you think this is fair? What qualities does Yoshi have that would serve him well as a samurai? What qualities do you think are important for a warrior to have?

3. Ozawa the painter tells Yoshi that a paintbrush is more likely to stop conflict than swords. What does Ozawa mean by this? Are there moments in the story where this sentiment proves true?

4. When Jack tells off Toley for bullying Willis, he points out that friendship is different from intimidation. Jack says, "Why don't you ask him what he wants to do, instead of telling him what he wants to do?" How does this theme relate to the larger plot happening around him?

5. Each section of the book (and many of the chapters) opens with an epigraph, a quotation that relates to what follows. Choose an epigraph in the book that is meaningful to you. How does it relate to the section or chapter that follows it?

6. Jack leaves the ship on a whim and finds himself wandering through the unfamiliar woods of Japan. What does he notice, and how does the author's prose transport the reader into the scene?

7. Yoshi tries to sell his pictures of the Americans, but his customers complain when the images don't depict the foreigners as hairy or ugly. In response, Yoshi changes his images to fit what his customers want to see. How could this action be harmful? Have you seen instances where this kind of alteration happens in the present day?

8. Manjiro recites for Yoshi the American motto "E pluribus unum," which is Latin for "Out of many, one." How does Manjiro explain this saying? What does the phrase mean to you?

9. The book includes traditional Japanese paintings as well as journal excerpts from the America expedition that actually visited Japan in 1853. Materials like these are called "primary

sources," which means that they were created during the time period being written about or studied. How do these primary sources contribute to your reading experience?

10. Since the Japanese and American customs that show respect or friendship are different, several misunderstandings arise. What is the result of these misunderstandings, and could they have been avoided? How does knowledge of foreign customs help or make lives better for characters in the story?

11. When Yoshi and Jack meet again in America as young men, they talk about the political turmoil and the resulting violence happening in Japan. The men who are revolting are afraid of change and afraid of losing their culture. But are there other ways to react to change? Is it possible to keep important traditions while still adopting new ones? What are some ways societies can preserve what is important?

12. "Dramatic irony" is when the reader knows more than the characters in a story do. During Jack and Yoshi's conversation in America, the author uses the situation in Japan to allude to something similar that will occur in America without actually naming the event. What clues does the author provide, and how did it feel when you put them together?

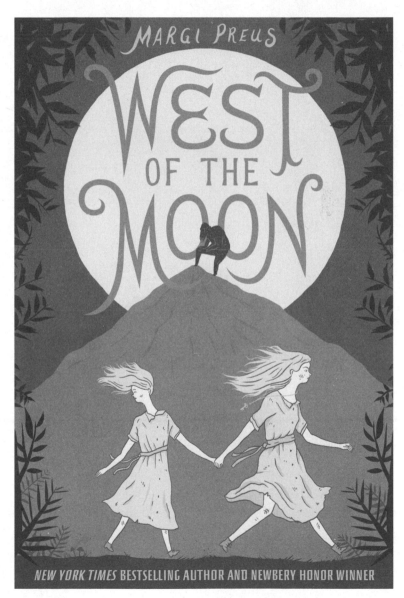

White Bear King Valemon

The fire hisses, then snaps, and the dog looks up from his place on the hearth. His hackles rise; a low growl escapes him. Aunt looks up from her knitting. A hush falls on the room—that curious feeling of something-about-to-happen seizes us. As for my cousins, the eldest holds her needle in midair; the middle one falls quiet, taking her hands away from the loom and setting them in her lap. The twins are silent, for once.

And me? Somewhere deep within me, my heart pounds, distant as an echo, as if it is already far away, in another place and another time.

There's a story I know about a white bear who came and took the youngest daughter away with him, promising the family everything they wanted and more, if the father would only let him take her. In the story, the family was sitting in their house when something passed by outside the window. Hands to their hearts, they all gasped. Pressed up against the window was the face of a bear—a white bear—his wet nose smearing the glass, his eyes searching the room. As he moved past, it was as if a splotch of sunlight momentarily penetrated the gloom.

That is *that* story. In *my* story I am sitting in the house with my aunt and uncle and cousins when something passes by outside the window. In the twilight it is just a dark shape. The room dims as the shadow goes by, and even after it passes, the darkness lingers, as if the sun has gone for good.

Aunt sets her knitting in her lap. She tries not to smile, holding her lips firm, but the smile makes its way to her forehead, and her eyebrows twitch with satisfaction.

My stomach works its way into a knot; my breath catches halfway down my throat.

A sharp knock on the door makes us all jump. Aunt gets up, smooths her skirt, and crosses to open it. My cousins glance at me, then away when I return their look. Greta isn't here. She must be hiding, which is just as well.

The man has to stoop to come in the low doorway, then, when inside, unfolds himself, but something makes him seem still stooped. It's a hump on his back. Even standing up straight it's there, like a rump roast oddly perched on one shoulder. I can't stop staring at it. He's chesty like an old goat, and wiry everywhere else. He's got the billy goat's scraggly beard and mean little eyes like black buttons. As ill-mannered as a goat, too, for he doesn't bother to take off his hat.

He squints around the room with his glittery eyes without saying *"God dag"* or *"Takk for sist."* No, his jaw works away at his cud of tobacco, and when he finally opens his mouth to reveal his stained teeth, it's to bleat out, "Which is the girl, then?"

His beady eyes gleam as they drift over pretty Helga's curves, glint as they take in Katinka's blonde braids, almost sparkle when they behold Flicka's ruddy cheeks. But when Aunt points to me, he turns his squint on me and his eyes turn flat and dark. "Well, I hope she can work," he grunts.

"Aye," says Aunt. "She's as hearty as a horse."

"Her name?"

"Astri."

"How old?"

"Thirteen. Fourteen by summer."

"Not a handful, I hope," he says. "I don't care for trouble in a girl. Don't care for it!" This he proclaims with a shake of his shaggy head and a stamp of his walking stick.

"She'll be no trouble to you, Mr. Svaalberd," Aunt lies. "Get your things, Astri."

My limbs are so numb I can barely climb the ladder into the loft. There is Greta, sitting on the lump of my straw mattress, her face wet with tears.

"Little sister," I say softly, and we embrace. I'd been able to keep from crying till now, when I hear her trembling intake of breath. "Greta," I whisper, "stop crying. Don't make me cry. I can't show Mr. Goat any weakness. You show a billy goat you're afraid of him, and he'll be lording it over you day and night."

Greta stops sniffling and takes my hands. "Big sister," she says, "you must be stronger—and meaner—than he is!"

"Aye, that's so," I say. "I shall be." I dry her tears with my apron and swipe at my own, too.

Her tiny hands press something into mine, something heavy, wrapped with a child's clumsiness in a piece of cloth. "You take this, Astri," she says.

I unwrap it to see our mother's silver brooch. "Keep it," Greta whispers. "Aunt will take it away if she finds out about it, you know."

I nod. Greta is already so wise for such a tiny thing. Too wise, maybe.

"Little sister," I tell her, holding my voice steady, "Papa will send for us, and then we'll go to America to join him."

Greta drops her head and nods. She doesn't want me to see she's crying, but her shoulders are shaking.

"Astri!" Aunt yells up the stairs. "Don't dawdle!"

I kiss the top of Greta's head and place my hand on her face for just a moment—all I dare, or risk a broken heart.

Down the ladder I go to stand by the door, my bundle under my arm. I can't help but notice there are now two shiny coins glinting on the table, along with a large, lumpy package. My cousins are eyeing the coins with the same intensity that the dog is sniffing the package. Now I know how much I'm worth: not as much as Jesus, who I'm told was sold for thirty pieces of silver. I am worth two silver coins and a haunch of goat.

Uncle comes and tucks a wisp of hair behind my ear, almost tenderly. "I'm sorry, Astri," he says. "It can't be helped."

That's all there is for a good-bye, and then out the door I go.

I n the story, the young maid climbed upon the white bear's back, and he said, "Are you afraid?"

No, she wasn't.

"Have you ever sat softer or seen clearer?" the white bear asked.

"No, never!" said she.

Well. That is a story and this is my real life, and instead of White Bear King Valemon, I've got Old Mr. Goat Svaalberd. And instead of "Sit on my back," he says "Carry my bag," and on we troop through the darkening woods, the goatman in front and me behind, under the weight of his rucksack and my own small bundle of belongings. The only thing white is the snow—falling from the sky in flakes as big as mittens. Strange for it to be snowing already, while leaves are still on the trees. It heaps up on them, making the branches droop, and piles up on the goatman's hump until it looks like a small snowy mountain growing out of his back.

"Aren't you afraid of the trolls who come out at night?" he says.

"I'm not afraid," I tell him, though it's a lie. It's twilight; the sun has slipped behind the mountains, and the shadows begin to dissolve into darkness. The time of day when honest, churchgoing people go home to bed.

He breaks off a rowan twig and gives it to me. "Tuck that into your dress," says he, "for protection."

I stumble along behind the goatman, trying to memorize every boulder and tree, every bend in the trail so I can find my way back. But evening is ending and the full night is coming on. We leave a dotted line of footprints behind us, which are rapidly filled in with snow. By morning there won't be a trace of us left behind.

✳✳✳

When the youngest daughter arrived at the bear's house, it was a castle she found, with many rooms all lit up, rooms gleaming with gold and silver, a table already laid, everything as grand as grand could be. Anything she wanted, she just rang a little silver bell, and there it was.

Not so for me, for when I come to the lair of Mr. Goat, it is a hovel, and filthy inside. The walls are soot-covered, and the fireplace so full of cinders that every time the door opens or shuts, ashes and smoke puff out into the room, enough to make you choke. A hard lump—ash, I suppose—settles in my throat.

The goatman's dog—Rolf, his name is—plunks himself down on the hearth and trains his yellow eyes on me.

Old Goatbeard lights a smoky fire in the fireplace and dumps a cold, greasy hunk of mutton on the table. Then he saws off the heel of a loaf of bread with a big, wide-bladed knife—the only thing shiny in the whole place, polished clean by the bread it slices.

When I scowl at the bread, he says, "Oh, a princess, are we? I suppose you're accustomed to pork roast and applesauce every night."

I say no, for of course we never had any such thing and most of the time no mutton, either, but at least our table was clean and what bread we had wasn't gray with ash and covered with sooty fingerprints.

With the last bit of bread, I swallow the lump that's been stuck in my throat. It slides down and lodges in my chest, where it stays, a smooth, cold stone pressed next to my heart.

Now it is time to sleep, and the goatman shows me my little bed in the corner.

Never trust a billy goat, Astri!

I know it, and so when Svaalberd goes outside to the privy, I sneak quietly to the table and take the heavy knife with the gleaming blade. Lacking the silken pillows with gold fringe that the girl got at King Valemon's castle, I tuck my own little bundle under my head. And under the bundle I slide the knife.